# Mr. Revere and I

# Mr REVERE and I

*Being an Account of certain
Episodes in the Career of*
## PAUL REVERE, *Esq.*
*as recently revealed by his Horse,*
## SCHEHERAZADE,
*late Pride of his Royal Majesty's
14th Regiment of Foot*

\* \* \* \* \* \* \* \*

Set down and Embellished with
Numerous Drawings by
## ROBERT LAWSON

\* \* \* \* \* \*

A YEARLING BOOK

Published by
DELL PUBLISHING CO., INC.
1 Dag Hammarskjold Plaza
New York, New York 10017
Copyright 1953, by Robert Lawson
For information address
Little, Brown and Company,
Boston, Massachusetts 02106.
Yearling ® TM 913705, Dell Publishing Co., Inc.
Reprinted by arrangement with
Little, Brown and Company
Printed in the United States of America
Fourth Dell Printing—December 1978

MPC

# Contents

# Mr. Revere and I

## 1. Pride of the 14th

How times and fortunes do change! It is difficult for me to realize that I am at present leading a life of rustic simplicity in the quiet pasture of one Paul Revere, merchant, on the outskirts of the City of Boston — just an ordinary farm horse called "Sherry." Not that I have any real cause for complaint: my circumstances are most comfortable, my duties almost none.

But sometimes one cannot help thinking back, a bit wistfully, to past glories and bygone triumphs.

To think that I, Scheherazade, once the most admired mount of the Queen's Own Household Cavalry, onetime toast of the Mustardshire Fencibles, late pride of His Royal Majesty's 14th Regiment of Foot, should be reduced to such a commonplace existence is somewhat saddening.

Would that some understanding historian could relate my story fittingly, but there being none available I must make shift to tell in my own way the trail of events resulting in my vastly changed estate.

It all started with the imbecile, practically sacrilegious, determination of these stubborn Colonists to defy the sacred authority of our Royal and Sovereign Majesty King George III.

Well do I remember that Monarch's regal presence on the occasion of our last review before leaving England. It is perhaps true that he might have made a more impressive appearance if mounted on a spirited charger, instead of being encased in a wicker wheel chair with his foot propped up on a particularly hideous cushion. This was made necessary by a severe attack of gout, an ailment highly fashionable at the moment. Nevertheless, about his brow there glowed the aura of magnificence, as with a languid motion of the hand His Majesty acknowledged the march-past of our Regiment.

It was the most thrilling moment of my entire military career. I was curried and brushed to a satiny glow. My hoofs were

4

Left.<sup>nt</sup> Sir Cedric
Noel Vivian
Barnstable

RL

freshly oiled, my mane braided with ribbons. My harness was saddle-soaped and rubbed, my brasses glittered. As I caracoled and stepped high to the blare of the band and the roar of the kettledrums, I feel sure there was no mount present more admired than I. Certainly there was none more filled with military ardor and pride in the glory of His Majesty's armed might.

On this memorable occasion my rider, and owner, was Leftenant Sir Cedric Noel Vivian Barnstable, Bart., a Gentleman and Officer in the highest tradition of British Arms. My Leftenant was the perfect picture of the ideal Military Man. Just turned twenty-one, tall and slender (not spindly, as some said), he had the true proud nose of the conqueror, rather like that of a puffin, but less elaborately colored. He was blessed with splendid strong teeth not greatly different from my own. These were quite prominently displayed, because his mouth was usually partly open and his chin was merely a slight ripple in the flesh, a highly prized characteristic of the Barnstable family.

A fall from his nurse's arms at the age of two had resulted in a continual and somewhat copious watering of his pale blue eyes and had also left him with a slight speech impediment. It was not quite a stammer or a stutter but more a combination of the two.

On this morning of our great review my master, unfortunately, was nine tenths asleep. There had been a farewell dinner for our officers the previous night, which had lasted well into the morning. My Leftenant, who required at least ten hours' sleep

to stay awake at all the next day, was having a terrible time keeping his eyes open. However, as I was far more familiar with the various evolutions than he, I performed them all faultlessly and his condition passed unnoticed.

Leftenant Barnstable was aide-de-camp to Sir Dagmore Dalrymple, Colonel of the 14th and commander of our expedition. This morning the poor Colonel was equally sleepy, and during the Blessing of the Colours by the Archbishop of Stilton he not only fell sound asleep but snored loudly. His mount, a handsome charger named Ajax, possessed a remarkable sense of balance and was most adroit at keeping the Colonel aboard under such circumstances; but the snores annoyed the Bishop no end, and Ajax was deeply mortified.

Within a day or two the expedition was embarked — in most uncomfortable quarters, I must say. Our force consisted of the 14th and 29th Regiments of Foot and a detachment of the 59th with two fieldpieces.

Our purpose, according to the Sealed Orders (which the Lord Privy Seal had forgotten to seal) was to occupy the Port of Boston in the Massachusetts Colony.

Here we were to uphold the authority of the Royal Governor and the Crown, to put down the disorders in which these unruly louts were constantly indulging, to make safe His Majesty's military stores, and at all times to comport ourselves with the valor and dignity of true English Gentlemen and Soldiers of the King.

I will not dwell long on the horrors of that trip. It was my first sea voyage, but Ajax, who had made several, said he had seen worse. What *they* could have been like I cannot imagine, for it is hard to conceive of any voyage being worse than ours.

We were quartered in the hold of an extremely old and leaky vessel misnamed the *Glorious*. There was no light and less air. Our hay was moldy, the grain mildewed and weevily, the water unspeakable. Rats were everywhere; they ate the food from under our very noses, they nibbled at our hoofs, they made sleep impossible. Our stalls were never cleaned, and of course currying and brushing were unheard-of.

Our grooms occupied the deck above us and a worse lot could scarce be imagined. They had been plucked from the gaols and prisons to fill out our ranks and fought and caroused unceasingly. Ajax and I were fortunate, for the thug assigned to

8

us had been in prison for horse stealing, so at least he knew *something* of horses, and we fared a bit better than our less lucky companions.

How we envied the artillery horses who were stabled on the open deck of another transport, the *Unfathomable!* Of course they were exposed to the weather, and three were swept overboard in a storm; but I think I envied those three most of all.

From the conversation of the so-called grooms, we learned the make-up of the rest of the expedition. There were four transports for the troops, whose condition was not much better than ours, except that they were given rum three times a day and were allowed to go on deck now and then, weather permitting. They had to be closely watched, however, for many had shown a most unpatriotic tendency to jump overboard. A very fine ship,

RL

the *Thunderous,* was given over entirely to the Officers and their servants; and of course we had an escort of four great ships of the line: the *Implacable,* the *Incapable,* the *Impossible* and the *Implausible.*

Our passage consumed only a little more than one month — remarkably fast, Ajax said, but to me it seemed an endless horror. Had I been capable of any feeling at all I should have rejoiced when, on the last day of September, 1768, the everlasting motion stopped and the roaring of the anchor chains shuddered through the ship. As it was, I was too sick and weary to care. I could not be interested when the grooms stumbled below to throw us our horrid evening meal.

We were anchored in Boston Harbor, I gathered. Tomorrow we would land. All troops to be clean-shaven, belts pipe-clayed, arms and accoutrements polished, uniforms pressed, hair powdered . . .

There was no mention of us horses.

## 2. Welcome to Boston

NEXT MORNING, October first, the ship was astir long before daybreak. From the unusual amount of tramping and cursing and the unfamiliar smell of soap and water we judged that the grooms were shaving, washing and donning clean uniforms.

Shortly after sunrise the hatches were removed and I thought my heart would burst for joy. After a month or more of darkness, to see once again the blue sky, the gleaming white clouds, to breathe in the crisp clear October air that filtered down to our noisome dungeon! Overhead sea gulls wheeled and chattered; Ajax even managed to toss his head and whinny weakly. I am afraid that I shed a few tears.

We could hear the creaking of the falls as the boats were lowered, and from the bumping and the shouted orders knew that our soldier grooms were being ferried ashore. We had not been fed or watered.

Sometime later the *Glorious* was towed in, made fast to a wharf, and we were hoisted ashore. Ordinarily there is nothing more humiliating than to have a canvas sling passed under one's middle, to be hoisted up to the yardarm like a sack of grain and then lowered to the ground. But this time the indignity was lost in the overpowering thrill of release from that horrible ship.

What joy it was to feel the solid earth again under one's feet, to feel the warm sun on one's back, even though the earth seemed to sway and rock and the sunlight almost blinded us.

And to really eat! There were buckets of fresh spring water, a cartload of sweet-smelling meadow hay, baskets of clean oats. After my first edible meal in weeks I felt refreshed enough to survey our surroundings with some slight interest.

Rising up from the water on some unimpressive hills, the town of Boston looked pleasant enough, but countrified and flimsy compared to our English cities. While there were a good many presentable brick buildings, the majority were constructed of wood, many of them unpainted. The streets were rambling, muddy and filled with puddles. Most of them seemed mere cowpaths. There appeared to be an unnecessarily large number of church spires.

The Long Wharf had been cleared of civilians and was now all abustle with our troops, who were still landing from small boats. Around the head of the wharf and all up the street leading to it stood a great crowd of townspeople. Stupid rustic bumpkins they seemed to be, somewhat sullen, but quiet and orderly.

Then I looked about at my companions, and a sorry looking company we were. Our coats were long and shaggy, matted with straw and filth, our hoofs rat-gnawed, our ribs and hipbones protruding painfully, heads hanging. Many could not stand at all; those who could stand, just could.

Soon Colonel Dalrymple arrived to inspect us. He was accompanied by several Officers, one of whom was my Leftenant, Sir Cedric Barnstable. As Sir Dagmore surveyed our pitiful state his jowls grew purple with rage.

"Who has had charge of these mounts?" he demanded. A Sergeant shambled forward and saluted.

"Fifty lashes," the Colonel roared, "and demoted to the ranks."

"Fif- fif- fif- fif . . ." Sir Cedric stammered, writing it down in a notebook.

"Egad, we cawn't ride those scarecrows," the Colonel sputtered. "We shall have to walk."

"Wa- wa- wa . . . ?"

13

"Yes walk, march, proceed on foot," Sir Dagmore shouted. "All Officers will proceed on foot. FORM RANKS!"

"For- for- for- FORM . . . Ra- ra- ra- RANKS," the Leftenant repeated.

Weak and weary though I was, it made my heart leap with pride to see how quickly and efficiently our troops fell into formation. Crossbelts gleaming white against their scarlet coats, buttons all aglitter, hair powdered, queues neatly tied, muskets and bayonets shining clean, they formed a stirring picture indeed. The only thing that at all marred the impressiveness was a vigorous and incessant scratching among all ranks. Those transports had been far from sanitary.

A small delegation of the town's officials had arrived and were being angrily questioned by the Colonel on the strange and unexplained absence of the Royal Governor, Francis Bernard.

"Most unusual, most unusual," Sir Dagmore sputtered. "Most inconsiderate — downright rude. Should be here to welcome us, should be here."

"Frankie's gawn upcountry fishin'," a lanky rustic bawled from the crowd. "Reckin he doan't like the smell o' Bawstin naow."

Looking his most imposing, the Colonel drew himself up and faced the townspeople.

"Now then, now then . . ." he commanded in his best parade-ground voice. "We are all loyal subjects of the Crown, I take it. We will have three cheers for His Majesty the King. *Hip- hip —* "

Except for the chattering and mewing of the sea gulls there was complete silence.

14

"Hip- hip — " From somewhere in the crowd there came a shrill and surprisingly realistic *"Cock-a-doodle-doo."* "Hip-hip — " roared Sir Dagmore a third time. A youth's raucous voice answered: "Yah — Lobster-backs — lobster-backs! Go peddle yer lobsters!"

"Lobster" of course referred to a nasty sort of marine crustacean much esteemed by these yokels as a food. When plunged into a pot of boiling water the shells of these creatures turn a brilliant red, not unlike the coats of our troops. At the moment the Colonel's jowls were a remarkably similar hue, but with great dignity he placed himself at the head of the column and gave the command to march.

The fifes shrilled, the drums thundered, the banners rippled in the afternoon sun, the boots of the troops rose and fell steadily. Ajax arched his neck, stamped his hoofs and almost tore loose from his picket rope. While I had not the strength to display this much spirit, my heart did leap at the sight of the rigid ranks of my Regiment advancing up the hill with such absolute and irresistible precision.

But I seethed with rage at hearing, instead of the thunderous applause and cheers which usually greeted us, only an occasional jeer of . . . "Yah, yah! Bloody-backs — bloody-backs! 'Oo wants lobsters?"


The fresh air, the sun, the food and water, did wonders in restoring our strength and spirits. By evening most of the horses were able to stand.

"A few days in comfortable stables and we'll be in tiptop shape," Ajax said. "I don't see why they don't hurry up and get us there though. Very poor management I must say, very poor."

It was after sunset and the air was becoming chilly before a new Sergeant and several grooms arrived and led us up through the town. We were a sorry sight, I am sure, as we stumbled weakly over the uneven streets and through the mud puddles.

"See you've brung your vittles with you," a voice bawled from the twilight. "How much for the hoofs and hides?"

"Go fry yer ears," the Sergeant bawled back, "you clam-eating yahoos!"

Alas for Ajax's hopes for a comfortable stable! It seemed that these churlish peasants, instead of welcoming His Majesty's Forces to good well-equipped quarters, had impudently refused them entrance everywhere. My Regiment, the 14th, had finally secured shelter in a drafty building called Faneuil Hall; but the 29th, the Artillery, and, of course, we horses, were forced to remain in the open, camped on a desolate strip of land known as Boston Common.

The night was chilly; the soldiers, clustered around makeshift campfires, continued to scratch. But we had no fires, no blankets, no stalls, no bedding. Glad though we were to be ashore, I must say that our welcome to His Majesty's Loyal Colony of Massachusetts could scarcely be called heart-warming.

## 3. Officers, Gentlemen and Bumpkins

This intolerable state of affairs
was soon set right by our intrepid Commander. In little more
than a month, Colonel Dalrymple's roaring and sputtering and
Leftenant Barnstable's stuttering and stammering had secured

18

possible quarters for the troops and horses — at outrageous rentals, it may be added. We were all deeply grateful, for by mid-November the weather had become extremely cold and unpleasant.

On the night of our arrival our Officers had taken over a fairly comfortable tavern called "the King's Arms." That is, it was called that when we arrived, but these unmannerly Patriots soon took to pelting the inn sign with oystershells, fish heads and other unpleasant missiles, many of which, missing their mark, crashed through the windows, causing considerable disturbance. Thereupon the host, although a stanch Loyalist, wisely altered the sign and renamed his hostelry "the Liberty Belle."

Ajax and I were quartered in the inn stables, which were somewhat crude and drafty, but on the whole comfortable enough. Of course they were a sad comedown from the accommodations to which we had been accustomed in England, but after those foul transports none of us felt moved to complain.

Our food, moreover, was delicious and abundant. I must admit that these churlish peasants did raise excellent hay and grain, although the Royal Paymaster used to roar with pain at the prices he was charged. So exorbitant were they that he was scarcely able to put aside more than 50 per cent of the disbursements for himself.

In the matter of food our masters were less fortunate. Sir Dagmore Dalrymple suffered especially in this respect, for he was accustomed to roast beef at least three or four times a day and here in this desolate country beef was almost impossible to obtain. Cattle were extremely scarce and the peasantry preferred to save them for their own use. Only on very rare occasions was it possible to secure an old and infirm cow that had been mangled by wolves or shot by Indian marauders. At such times, the Officers of our Regiment usually tendered a banquet to the Officers of the 29th. Sir Dagmore was invariably laid up for a week or more afterwards and many of the Officers injured their teeth severely by biting on Indian arrowheads.

With proper care and the good food, we horses rapidly regained our strength and spirits. Before long we really began to enjoy this strange new country, except for the weather — which was most violent, quite unlike our English climate.

That first fall and winter were exceptionally bitter; snow piled high in the streets, cold so sharp that one's muzzle was often coated with frost, winds that drifted the snows ever deeper.

Our Officers seldom ventured abroad, but stayed snugly indoors at the Liberty Belle, playing cards and sleeping. Sir Dagmore was especially accomplished at this; often, after one of the roast-beef gorges, sleeping for four or five days at a time.

Once in a while, if the weather was sunny, my Leftenant would come out to the stables to inspect us.

"Wa-wa-wa-well, Sh-Sh-Sh-Sherry old girl," he would cry, slapping my neck. "Thu-thu-thu-thumbs up, old dear. Bla-bla-bla-blawsted winter caw-caw-cawn't last f-f-f-f-forever. Ca-ca-ca-carry on."

By this time his eyes would be watering more profusely than ever and his nose would have assumed a pale bluish color. Wrapping his cloak more tightly about him he would dash the few feet from the stables to the warmth of the inn.

Ajax, stamping and tossing his head proudly, would say: "There, my girl, is a true Officer and Gentleman for you. How many ordinary common people would go to all that trouble to see to the welfare of their mounts? Gentlemen, my dear Scheherazade, are born, not made."

"How true, how true," I murmured, taking a kick at the groom who had just brought our water. I always admired Ajax for his profound thoughts and original observations.

The winter finally ended. There was a warm thaw; icicles fell from the eaves, the snowdrifts melted and ran down the streets in rivers of slush, the bare muddy ground of the Common reappeared.

Then suddenly it was full spring, with the trees bursting into leaf, birds singing, grass sprouting green. Our stables were cleaned out; the doors stood open, admitting the fresh warm air and sunshine. Our Officers emerged from their hibernation, and the Liberty Belle was given a thorough airing.

After his long rest Sir Dagmore Dalrymple was bursting with energy; all the younger Officers were as spirited as young colts let out of pasture. The common soldiers were marched down to the Harbor and given their spring bath.

We had daily parades now through the almost dry streets of the city. The troops were spick-and-span, their buttons and buckles worn thin by the long winter's idleness, during which they had had nothing to do *but* polish buttons and buckles.

It was tremendously thrilling to be once more stepping along at the head of the column of our splendid men, with the drums roaring and the fifes shrilling.

The only thing that marred the pleasure of these occasions was the fact that our fine display was completely ignored by the churlish townspeople. They merely clumped stolidly along about their petty businesses, never even turning heads to glance

at us. In fact, many very pointedly turned their backs as we approached, a piece of impudence which always caused Sir Dagmore to turn purple with rage. No longer did they even bother to shout insults, and only very occasionally was a dead fish or a vegetable thrown.

Made furious by this studied indifference, our Commander ordered parades every Sunday morning before all their churches or meetinghouses, with the fifes and drums playing their loudest. Even this failed to impress these stubborn malcontents. Completely unmoved, they continued to wail their dismal hymns and shout their endless sermons, though the fifers blew themselves breathless.

As the weather grew more summery we began to enjoy many delightful rides in the country surrounding Boston. Our high-spirited young Officers liked nothing better than a jolly picnic at some rustic spot such as Roxbury, Dorchester or Cambridge. Very often a group of five or six, accompanied by a cart full of food and wine and a squad of orderlies to do the serving, would sally forth to spend a pleasant day fishing, swimming, running

races, playing at hopscotch or rounders and occasionally shooting at the rustics' poultry. They were also shot at occasionally by
the rustics, but took it all in the spirit of good fun.

Thanks to these expeditions, and our hunting parties in the
autumn, I learned a great deal about the surrounding countryside. I became thoroughly familiar with every settlement, road

and lane — a knowledge which was to prove of utmost value to me later.

Unfortunately, in the city the social life of the Officers was sadly limited. While many of the better families were Loyalists and possessed handsome residences excellently suited to entertaining, none of them dared to be seen even speaking to an Officer of the King.

The few who did venture to invite an Officer for tea or dinner promptly discovered their windows broken, their lawns piled high with lobster shells and their doors and fences defaced with insulting and threatening placards. These notices were always signed by "the Sons of Liberty," a rebellious organization of low-class ruffians and ne'er-do-wells who were causing an infinite amount of disorder, in a sneaky underhand way.

This state of affairs was a particular hardship for my Leftenant Barnstable, who was a highly accomplished dancer and loved nothing better than a genteel ball or rout. It left him with no alternative save to spend his leisure time at cards and dice in the taverns. As he was a notoriously bad card player and his luck at dice was even more unfortunate, I viewed his activities with grave misgivings, misgivings which were shortly to prove only too well founded.

## 4.  Pride Goeth before . . .

Almost every Sunday we had
horse racing on the Common. The troops had constructed a race
track of sorts that encircled the entire area. Of course it was
rough and crude, not to be compared to our beautiful velvet-
green English tracks. In fact it was more like a cross-country or
steeplechase course.

It must be admitted that the race meets were somewhat noisy.
But since their main purpose was to annoy the townspeople, who
disapproved of horse racing at any time and considered it doubly

26

wicked on Sunday, our Officers did nothing to discourage the noise. The course was always lined with soldiers and a great many sailors from the guard ships in the Harbor. Tremendous amounts of money were wagered, excitement ran high and fights were frequent. In fact, each meet usually ended in a small riot as the troops of the 14th battled those of the 29th, and the sailors battled everyone in sight.

Without wishing to appear unduly boastful I must say that I was quite the fastest horse of our Forces. Moreover, Leftenant Barnstable was a splendid horseman and very lightweight, despite his tallness. Ajax, of course, was magnificent, but built more for endurance than speed, while his Colonel Dalrymple, who weighed a full fifteen stone, made a formidable handicap. A bay mare, Mildred, owned by Colonel Carr of the 29th, was very fleet of foot and my closest rival. Had she been less temperamental she might have proved a great racer, but she was more than apt to be sulky and refuse to run at all or else flighty and completely uncontrollable.

It gave me the greatest pleasure to win so many of these races for my Leftenant, as it was clear that he sorely needed the money. His losses at cards were prodigious and he was deeply in debt — which, of course, was usual and proper for a young Officer and Gentleman of His Majesty's Armed Service, but caused me some concern.

Of course the better-class Colonists ignored our race meets completely, but a certain number of rough characters, mostly Sons of Liberty, did congregate in the vicinity of the Common where they could watch from a distance and doubtless make bets among themselves. As real money was very scarce among them, these wagers seemed to consist chiefly of sacks of turnips, baskets of eggs and such lowly produce.

One of the leaders of this group was a loud-mouthed ne'er-do-well whom they called Sam Adams. He did no betting, for he did not own even a sack of turnips. Nor was he interested in the races, only in talking. Mounted on an upturned market basket, he would rant and roar by the hour, mouthing idiotic phrases about Liberty, Taxes, Tyranny, Acts of Parliament and other subjects rightly the concern of his betters. He would keep up this ridiculous performance until his audience tired of it and left, or one of his creditors, of whom he seemed to have a great many, appeared. Whereupon he would dismount from his basket and beat a hasty retreat.

This rebellious impudence used to make Ajax furious. "By gad," he would snort — "should put a stop to that. The rascal ought to be thrown in jail. 'Pon my word I don't know what things are coming to."

However, our authorities felt it more dignified merely to ignore such a preposterous demagogue and did nothing to curb his disloyal activities. In my humble opinion this was a great mistake, but of course my opinion was never asked.

Our greatest race and, alas, my final one, took place on Sunday the twelfth of September, 1770, a date that will live forever in my mind. For it marked a great change in my fortunes and circumstances.

28

This was a gala occasion in honor of His Majesty's Birthday — which actually occurred in January but was always celebrated in September because the weather was usually better then. Since the previous day had been pay day for the troops and for the Fleet, and since all had been given an extra ration of rum to drink the King's Health, the occasion promised to be unusually gala — and noisy.

Our two field guns had roared out a Royal Salute of twenty-seven rounds (and two misfires); the drummers and fifers played "God Save the King" quite accurately considering their condition. A few members of the Council had been persuaded to lend their presence. Even a handful of the wealthier Loyalists had dared the disapproval of their neighbors and attended, dressed in their finest.

The main event was the race for the King's Cup, a handsome punch bowl, made by one Paul Revere, a local silversmith. Several horses had been entered, but the only three who really counted were Ajax and I and that silly little Mildred of the 29th.

With pay day only a few hours gone, huge amounts had been wagered — especially among the Officers. I was particularly determined to win, for my Leftenant, Sir Cedric, had plunged more heavily than most, all of his bets being I.O.U's or promises to pay. To lose would mean nothing short of a calamity for him.

The race was twelve furlongs, a bit over twice around the track. After a rather confused start, Ajax and I quickly pulled well out in front of the pack; then I settled down to an easy pace, for I did not like to leave poor old Ajax too far behind. Mildred, made giddy by all the crowds and attention, was showing off disgracefully and giving her Colonel Carr a thoroughly unhappy time.

It was not until we had made a circuit-and-a-half of the track, and were approaching the home stretch, that she dropped her silly play-acting and came racing up like a spiteful whirlwind. Much as I hated to desert the faithful Ajax, I had to really let myself out now to keep this little upstart in her place. I must admit she could truly run, once she had set her mind to it, but I was quite able to maintain a lead of a full length.

Then, as the finish line loomed up only a few yards away, with certain victory only a matter of seconds — disaster struck!

On the edge of the Common nearest to a miserable little lane called Joy Street stood that reprobate Sam Adams and a gang

of his jeering rowdies. As we passed, one of them scaled a large jagged-edged oystershell in our direction. As misfortune would have it this vicious missile, curving in a long sweeping arc, caught me directly across the bridge of the nose.

Naturally I shied — who could help doing so? At this terrific pace a shy meant a stumble and as I stumbled Ajax's shoulder bumped my withers. I fell, a clumsy sprawling fall, tossing my poor Leftenant far over my head.

That nasty little Mildred capered over the line an easy winner. Ajax thundered in, a poor second, and some stupid horse of the 29th was third. A fine record for the proud 14th!

At once pandemonium broke forth. The enraged and disappointed troops of the 14th piled into the arrogant 29th. The sailors, who had placed bets on both sides, waded into the fray without discrimination. Fists thudded and belts slashed. The Sons of Liberty melted away into the shadows of Joy Street.

I had suffered a slightly strained shoulder, otherwise I was all right, although badly shaken up. Leftenant Barnstable was placed on a shutter and carried up to the Liberty Belle, while a groom led me limping to the stable.

Since our Regimental Surgeon was busied with the riot still raging on the Common, a civilian physician, one Dr. Warren, was summoned to examine the Leftenant. After a time he emerged with Sir Dagmore Dalrymple and they paused a moment in the inn courtyard.

"He should have complete rest," Dr. Warren said gravely. "Rest and careful observation. I greatly fear a brain injury. His responses are very vague and disconnected."

"Vague? Disconnected?" the Colonel roared. "Egad, he's *always* that way. Seemed brighter than usual to me."

My shoulder soon recovered, but my spirits did not. I was completely crushed and humiliated at the thought of my miserable failure. The Officers of the 14th, all of whom had lost large wagers, eyed me reproachfully, some with open contempt.

As for Leftenant Sir Cedric Barnstable, this final blow proved his complete undoing. Desperate now, to redeem his pledges of honor he plunged into still more frantic play at cards and dice. He even descended so far as to play with the natives, mostly at the Green Dragon Tavern, a low hostelry much frequented by those ruffianly Sons of Liberty. It was here one evening that my pride received its last crushing blow.

It was a miserably cold wet October night and I was hitched to the horse rail with no blanket or other protection. An east wind laden with drizzle blew in off the Harbor, causing my injured shoulder to ache horribly. Inside, through the smoky windows, I could see much activity around the gaming tables; now and then when the door was opened there drifted out snatches of song, laughter, oaths and a great deal of foul tobacco smoke.

Sometime after midnight my Leftenant stumbled forth, accompanied by a stout moon-faced citizen. I recognized him at once as one Nathaniel Sime, better known locally as "Stinky Nat," the proprietor of a noisome glue factory not far from the Common. My heart sank as this unsavory character untied my reins and prepared to mount.

"Gug-gug-gug-good-by, old girl," Sir Cedric cried. "Yu-yu-yu-you have a n-n-n-new owner. Thu-thu-thu-thumbs up! Blaw-blaw-blaw-blawsted luck's bub-bub-bub-bound to change su-su-su-sometime."

Then he sat down heavily on the curbstone and my new owner heaved himself into the saddle.

Of course this rude bumpkin was no horseman; I could have tossed him off as easily as a sack of grain. But naturally, for a horse of my breeding, this would never do. For one must never, never allow one's personal feelings to interfere in the perfect performance of one's horsely duties. Ajax expressed this so splendidly when he used to say, "After all, my dear, like 'im or not, your master is your master."

How I would miss dear Ajax and his wise counsel! As I stumbled miserably along through the black alleys my spirits reached their lowest ebb. And to make things even more depressing, there kept running through my mind the words of a horrid song that our grooms used to sing:

> *Old Horses never die,*
> *They only go to the glue factory.*

## 5. Less than the Dust

$\text{M}$Y NEW MASTER stabled me in a ramshackle shed in the rear of his glue factory, tossed in some shavings for bedding and left me. The stench from the factory was overpowering, but it did not seem to discourage the rats in the least. They were almost as thick as they had been on the transports.

Next morning I was taken in charge by one of the workmen, a creature even more repellent in appearance than Stinky Nat himself, if such a thing were possible. He bore the name of Hezekiah, but was always known as "Hezzy." In youth the Town Fathers had burned off the tip of his tongue for using profanity on a Sunday. This made his speech somewhat peculiar and his disposition even more so, but on the whole he was a rather harmless clodhopper and not too unkind to me.

This morning he hitched me to a clumsy two-wheeled cart and we clattered down to a fish wharf owned by one Benoni Pottle. While Hezzy busied around loading the cart with fish heads, skins, bones, and the other offal that went into the making of glue, Mr. Pottle eyed me with considerable interest.

"Nice-looking mare you got there," he finally said. "How'd Nat come by the likes of her?"

"Won her at dice off a lobster-back Officer," Hezzy mumbled.

"Humph, didn't know Nat had that much knack with the dice."

"Hain't," Hezzy guffawed, "but they was his dice."

He climbed to his seat and we trudged up through the town, where ladies delicately covered their faces with lace handkerchiefs and little boys held their noses and shouted insults as we passed.

In the afternoon we drove to the slaughterhouse, whence we fetched an equally offensive load of hoofs and horns. Then, apparently, my duties for the day were done. I was fed, rather poorly, watered and bedded down for the night. This was to be my daily routine for many months.

While the work was not unduly hard the humiliation was almost too dreadful to bear. In the first place, for a horse of my background and attainments to be put in harness at all was unthinkable. Had I my old strength and spirits I would have kicked cart and harness to bits before submitting to such an in-

dignity. Then to be hitched to a *cart,* and *such* a cart — its unsavory loads the butt of jeers and insults whenever it appeared on the streets!

Also there was my appearance, which grew steadily more pitiful. Nat Sime was not one to waste money on fancy feed,

37

so mine was both atrocious and scanty. I was always half shod, my coat grew long and matted. Hezekiah, although kindly enough, knew nothing of the care of horses. My stable was seldom cleaned; often he forgot to water me or give me bedding. I developed two collar sores which he did not know how to treat. They became more painful and hideous daily.

Worst of all was the constant dread that someday I would come face to face with my old Regiment. Changed though my appearance was, every horse would surely recognize me, and that would be the last straw; the very thought of it chilled me. I could picture the dismay of Ajax and the sneers of that nasty little Mildred. I resolved firmly that rather than undergo that ordeal I would first drown myself in the Harbor.

Of course in a town as small as Boston it was inevitable that someday I must encounter my old comrades in arms and one morning the very thing that I had been so dreading came to pass.

We were toiling up Milk Street from the wharfs with our usual load of gurry when I suddenly became aware of the familiar rattle of drums and the squealing of fifes. Raising my drooping head I beheld the proud van of the glorious 14th advancing down the hill in all its majesty. The morning sun winked and glittered on bayonet and buckle, the scarlet coats glowed hotly, the white-gaitered legs rose and fell rhythmically.

At the head, riding an unfamiliar horse, was Colonel Dalrymple; at his left rode Leftenant Sir Cedric Barnstable, mounted, of all things, on Ajax. Evidently his luck at cards had changed for the better. I had noted these things in a flash — then utter panic seized me! For the first time in my life I ran away.

Wheeling sharply I plunged into the first side street, my one thought to regain the docks and hurl myself into the Harbor waters. I did not get very far.

The street was a narrow one and almost blocked by a huge wain toiling up the hill. Cart and wagon locked wheels, then with a great crash the cart, I, Hezekiah and our horrid load piled up in a tangled mass on the sidewalk.

Almost at once a crowd gathered. A farrier, before whose shop the accident had occurred, came forth, cut the traces and helped me to my feet. I was only bruised but my nerves were completely shattered. I trembled in every limb.

Then I became aware of a familiar loud voice and saw the man they called Sam Adams approaching. There being no market basket handy he at once mounted the wreckage of the cart and began one of his speeches.

"Another outrage by these scarlet-coated minions of Tyranny," he shouted. "Not content to plant the iron foot of Oppression on our fair city they must even descend to frightening children and horses with their arrogant displays of ruthless military might. Who is the owner of this unfortunate steed?"

"B'longs to Nat Sime," Hezzy mumbled.

"Aha!" Adams roared, still louder. "Another stony-hearted oppressor. A known Loyalist, an enemy of the People. See, my friends, the pitiful condition of this abused, downtrodden half-starved beast. Does any wealthy, callous friend of Tyranny deserve to own and mistreat an equine slave such as this?"

There were angry mutters and cries of NO from the crowd. Adams called over the farrier and several of the onlookers.

39

"Look," he said in a low voice. "Paul Revere needs a horse badly for his duties; you all know what *they* are. This, I believe, is it. Leave it to me."

"She's a good horse," the farrier said. "Rested and cured up, she'll run with the best of them. I know real horseflesh."

Sam beckoned to six of the stoutest men in the crowd, shipyard workers mostly.

"By authority of the Committee of Correspondence," he announced, "I hereby appoint you a committee of six to at once

wait upon said Nathaniel Sime at his place of business. You will inform him that in the considered judgment of this meeting he, Nathaniel Sime, is not worthy of ownership of this abused and downtrodden horse. You will also inform him that aforesaid horse is, as of this moment, hereby expropriated by the afore-mentioned Committee of Correspondence, Boston, Chapter #1, and by the Sons of Liberty, for service in the advancement of Freedom, Equality and Independence — long may they prosper."

He directed a meaning look at the wagon spokes which littered the pavement. Each member of the Committee armed himself with one and the group marched off determinedly in the direction of the glue factory.

At this moment my poor nerves received a still greater shock and I almost collapsed amid the wreckage of the cart. For I heard a still more familiar voice. "Wha-wha-wha-what's gug-gug-gug-going on he-he-he-here?" it was saying.

I looked up, straight into the pale watery eyes of Sir Cedric Barnstable. Whether he recognized me or not I shall never know; I rather think he did, but if so he gave no sign of it. Then I turned my despairing gaze on Ajax.

*He* recognized me, of that I am positive, but there was no friendliness in his look as he eyed my sorry appearance with disdain. He looked at me and through me, then indifferently began to study the sign over the farrier's shop.

"Oh, Ajax!" I cried despairingly. "Surely *you* know me?"

"I never speak to civilians," he said coldly and continued to contemplate the sign.

"Whu-whu-whu-why don't you shoo-shoo-shoo-shoot the brute and gug-gug-gug-get it o-o-o-o-over with?" the Leftenant demanded.

"*Shoot the brute? What's going on here?*" roared Sam Adams. "This scarlet-coated, bedizened popinjay dares ask a group of honest citizens, peacefully assembled, *What's going on here?*"

"What-wha-wha-what's it to you, la-la-la-lobster-back?" mimicked a voice from the crowd. "He-he-he-here's what!" A very decayed codfish head hurtled through the air and took the Leftenant full in the chest. With a whole cartload of ammunition ready to hand, the Leftenant and Ajax at once became the target of a perfect shower of noisome missiles. Followed by jeers and catcalls, Leftenant Barnstable beat a hasty retreat toward Milk Street and his Regiment.

In my bitter humiliation and disillusionment I could not bring myself to feel any great regret for this disgraceful insult to the King's uniform.

Now, with the farrier leading me, we started off in the direction of Paul Revere's home. We formed quite a procession, Sam Adams on my right and the crowd marching along behind. Someone had draped a red, white and blue ribbon around my neck and I was enough recovered from my shock at least to hold up my head.

The Revere home was a modest but neatly kept house on North Street, near Love Lane. Attracted by the crowd, Mr. Revere emerged from his shop, followed by his wife, his mother and a perfect covey of children. He was a well-set-up man nearing forty and dressed in the usual garb of Colonial tradesmen. His fact lit up when he beheld me, although at the moment I could not have been much to look at.

"A horse," he cried happily. Sam Adams immediately mounted the horse block.

"Paul Revere," he began, "Citizen, Patriot, Son of Liberty, Mason, artist — and father: On behalf of the Committee of Correspondence, Boston, Chapter #1, on behalf of the Sons of Liberty and of these worthy citizens here assembled, it gives me the deepest pleasure to hereby present to you this magnificent steed, in order that you may still more efficiently carry on your noble efforts in the sacred cause of Liberty."

He seemed ready to go on indefinitely, but the crowd interrupted with a great cheer and the little Reveres all danced around singing, "Daddy's got a horsie, Daddy's got a horsie!"

Sam took Mr. Revere a little to one side. "Paul," he said in a lower voice. "That — er — little bill of yours, the one for silver shoe-buckles, you remember? Er — a bit overdue, I regret to say.

44

I was wondering if, in view of the present happy circumstances, you could, ahem, see your way clear to . . ."

Mr. Revere, who seemed unable to remove his fascinated gaze from me, interrupted. "Have you it with you?" he asked.

"I believe I have, somewhere," Sam Adams replied. He fumbled through his pockets, produced a large sheaf of bills and extracted from it an old and dog-eared piece of paper.

Mr. Revere, still with his eyes on me, absently took the bill, tore it into small bits and dropped them on the ground. "Consider it paid," he said smiling.

"There is the act of a true friend and Patriot, Paul," Sam cried happily. "On behalf of the Committee of Correspondence, Boston, Chapter #1, I thank you, on behalf of the Sons of Liberty I thank you, on behalf of my financially depressed wife and children I thank you, on behalf of myself I thank you. Now let's see about quarters for the horse."

Attached to the rear of the Revere house there was a small lean-to shed. Several carpenters and joiners offered their services for altering this into a stable.

"We need lumber," Sam Adams said, looking over the crowd. "You, Ebenezer Winslow, shall have the honor of furnishing the lumber for this worthy project."

"Who's paying for it?" the other countered warily. "Not you, I hope?"

"Posterity," Sam answered grandly.

"Don't know's I've ever heard the name," said Ebenezer, "but I'll take a chance on him."

All day the carpenters toiled with a will, and by evening had transformed the shed into a very snug little stable. One Patriot brought a cartload of hay, another several bushels of oats. The kindly farrier dressed my sores and promised to return the next day to clip me and see that I was properly shod. He showed the oldest Revere boy how to water and feed me and bed me down at night.

When all was finished he turned to Mr. Revere. "She'll come around fine," he said. "She'll be a horse to be proud of. She's got the lines and build. Can't fool me on horses. She'd better have two-three weeks' rest though."

"She'll have to," Paul Revere laughed. "You see, I've never yet been on a horse."

## 6. The Loving Family

I MUST SAY that the good farrier, for a Colonial bumpkin, did know his trade. He came almost daily to dress my collar sores, which healed rapidly; he shod me far better than our regimental farriers ever did; he got my hoofs in splendid shape; he clipped me beautifully. Within a week or two I began to look like my old self.

What was even more important was the tremendous improvement in my spirits and self-respect. This was due almost entirely to the loving attentions of the Revere family, especially the children, of whom, at the moment, there were six. Naturally in my military career I had never come in contact with young ones at all, and I will admit that I found them a great pleasure. They all adored me and were in and out of the stable continually. Paul, the only son, then thirteen, took entire charge of me. He kept my stall immaculate. He fed me regularly and bountifully. I had always an ample supply of fresh water from the pump in the back yard. He curried, brushed and rubbed me incessantly.

On pleasant sunny days I was given the freedom of the fenced-in back premises and often the three younger girls, Sarah, Frances and Mary, would be helped to my back and allowed to ride around the small yard at a sedate pace. Their shrieks of delight always brought the grownups out to watch the fun. Altogether it was a loving, kindly family and I could not help growing fond of them, even though they were only middle-class tradespeople — and, of course, rebellious Colonials.

Mr. Revere was being given riding lessons by various friends who owned horses — and, I understood, making good progress. He still had no saddle or bridle for me, but this was soon remedied. One Sunday evening Hezekiah from the glue factory arrived with a large gunny sack slung over his shoulder. He dumped it on the stable floor, grinning broadly as young Paul excitedly drew from it my old saddle and bridle. They smelled horribly of the factory, but Mr. Revere was delighted.

"Can't do much fer the Cause," Hezzy mumbled, "but here's these. Figgered Nat's got no use fer 'em. Got a ox to the cart now." He was amazed at my appearance, stroking my sleek neck and shoulders admiringly. "Don't reckin I was much of a groom," he admitted. "Oxes is more in my line." He departed, richer by a shilling and a clap on the shoulder from Mr. Revere.

48

There had been a window opening from the kitchen into the old shed, which was now my stable. This had not been closed up, so I was able to look into the kitchen and beyond it into the shop.

49

Since the kitchen was also the dining room and living room, I became, as it were, practically one of the family. My days and especially my evenings were now filled with new interest.

Mr. Revere was the busiest man I have ever seen. From dawn to dusk he worked in his shop, mostly hammering out very handsome pieces of silverware. But that was not all, by any means. He engraved many pictures on copperplates and from these plates made prints on paper. All of these were quite seditious: vulgar cartoons ridiculing His Majesty and his advisers. The most popular was a picture of that ridiculous little affray which they called "the Boston Massacre."

Whenever one of our Officers came in to order, perhaps, a pair of silver shoe-buckles, gold buttons or a snuffbox, Mr. Revere discreetly swept all these prints into a drawer. But other times they were boldly displayed and I was astonished at the number that were bought by the Patriots. Many of them, lacking money, paid with eggs, butter or other produce; but they always paid — which, I am ashamed to say, our Officers often did not.

In addition, Mr. Revere also carved many beautiful picture frames for his friend Mr. Copley, the great portrait painter. Strangest trade of all, he even made and fitted false teeth, an odd occupation for a silversmith, but with his large family no opportunity to earn an honest shilling could be neglected.

Evenings Mr. Revere was even busier and was almost never at home. He was a prominent Mason, a Fire Warden, a Son of Liberty, a member of the Caucus Club, the Long Room Club and any number of other organizations, all of them regrettably disloyal to King and Country. He attended their meetings almost nightly. On the few evenings that he remained at home, some of his friends were sure to drop in to talk politics and sedition: such men as John Hancock, Dr. Warren, James Otis and, of course, Sam Adams.

As for me, a loyal subject of His Majesty, some of the things that were said fairly made my blood boil; on the other hand, some of their arguments made many of their grievances seem quite justified. I was frightfully confused and upset. But who was I anyway, to concern myself with such matters? Only a horse, whose first duty is always to its master; and I had to admit that I now had the kindliest master ever a horse had, even though he was misguided.

It soon became clear that Mr. Revere's disloyal activities amounted to more than mere talk.

It happened on one of his rare evenings at home. Immediately the supper dishes were finished Mrs. Revere and the old lady departed, leaving him alone in the kitchen. He placed a candle at the window and within a few minutes there came a knock at the door. Great was my astonishment to see admitted a burly trooper of the 29th Regiment. For a moment I thought that perhaps he had come to arrest Mr. Revere, but he merely slumped wearily in a chair, then straightened up with a grimace of pain.

Mr. Revere passed the man a pipe and tobacco, lighted his own pipe and sat down on a stool by the fire. "Your name is Giles Treadwell, trooper, of the 29th Regiment of Foot?" he asked.

51

" 'Tis," the other answered.

"You are still determined?"

"Determined-er nor ever," the soldier answered. He suddenly leaped to his feet and with a growl of rage tore off his belt, crossbelts, scarlet coat and shirt. Then he turned, so that the light of the fire fell full on his back. Mr. Revere gave a gasp and I was fairly sickened at the sight. From shoulders to waist he was striped with angry red and purple welts raised the thickness of a man's finger, the skin caked with blackened, dried blood.

"All that," the man cried bitterly, "because I didn't salute a mincing Officer to suit his fancy taste. That spindly-legged, stuttering Leftenant it was, Sir Cedric Barnstable. Twenty-five lashes with the compliments of Sir Cedric, may his soul burn to black ashes. Have you ever felt the lash, sir?"

"No," Mr. Revere answered with a wry smile. "Here in America we are men, not beasts." He fetched a caldron of warm water, carefully washed the man's back and smeared it with a greasy ointment.

52

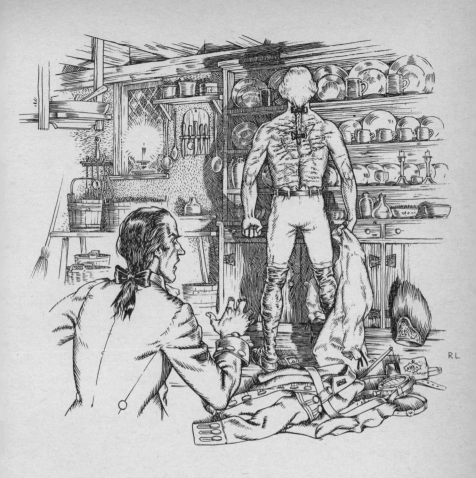

"What can you do on a farm?" he asked.

"Sheep," the other answered promptly. "I'll do anything gladly, but I'm handiest with sheep. I was said to be the best sheepman in our countryside before *they* got me drunk, gave me the King's shilling and pressed me into their beastly army."

"Good," Mr. Revere said. "Eben Doolittle in Medford is the

largest sheep raiser in these parts and needs good help. I have already spoken of you to him. Everything is arranged."

He fetched a pair of shears and cropped the man's hair roughly, in the manner of the countrymen. "Now wash the powder out of it," he directed.

While the trooper washed the powder out of his hair, restoring it to its natural light brown, Mr. Revere, rummaging in a chest, brought out a pair of heavy boots, woolen stockings, patched smallclothes, a faded smock and a broad-brimmed hat. When the man had stripped off the rest of his uniform and donned these, no trace of the soldier remained save the pile of scarlet and white clothes lying on the floor.

Mr. Revere surveyed the country bumpkin that he had created with considerable pride, then handed him a roughly drawn map showing the route to Medford. He explained this carefully, then said, "Now remember, your name is no longer Giles Treadwell of His Majesty's 29th Regiment of Foot. It is Enoch Sawtell, shepherd, of Medford. Stop standing straight and holding your shoulders back as you have been drilled to do — slouch. And *never* salute when spoken to — Americans never salute — or very seldom. Now be on your way, and all good fortune to you." The man wrung Mr. Revere's hand, his eyes brimming with gratitude, then stepped out into the night.

At once Mr. Revere snipped all the brass buttons, ornaments and buckles from the discarded uniform, weighed them and tossed them into a pot on the forge. The leather belts, cartridge boxes, shoes and gaiters were carefully rolled up and tied with a piece of twine. Mrs. Revere and the old lady appeared and were soon busy measuring and cutting the scarlet cloth, exclaiming over its handsome quality.

"The very finest red flannel," Mrs. Revere said happily. "Young Paul shall have new winter underwear and there may be enough to line Sarah's cape as well."

"Twenty ounces of good brass," Mr. Revere calculated. "Thomas the clockmaker pays eight shillings a pound for English brass. That is ten shillings. And Parr, the cobbler, will be glad to give five shillings for the leather; that makes fifteen shillings altogether."

"But Paul," his mother reproved, "you are not doing this for the money!"

"Of course not, Mother," he replied and smiled. "But we must eat and what could be pleasanter than to dine on the King's uniform?"

Within an hour there was no trace of the soldier's visit, save a melted-down bar of brass and a neat stack of cut-out pieces of cloth in Mrs. Revere's sewing basket.

I have lost count of how many times this traitorous performance was repeated; it seemed to occur every few evenings. Always there were the same pitiful tales of harsh and inhuman treatment, with which I could now thoroughly sympathize, goodness knows. Yet I had been brought up in the firm tradition that of all military crimes desertion was the very worst. I *should* have been horrified and outraged, but I could not be. I just became more confused and upset in my mind as time passed by.

Every few days some grinning countryman would appear at

the kitchen door bearing a heavy basket of vegetables, fruit or eggs; sometimes a chicken or two or a leg of mutton. They were all former soldiers of the King, all still eager to express their gratitude to Mr. Revere and his family. They were all now stanch Patriots. Most of them had joined the Colonial Militia, where their training made them most valuable. Enoch Sawtell the shepherd was now a Sergeant.

There were other Royal soldiers who were not contemplating desertion, but merely came to visit. Many were young countrymen torn from their homes and families. Stationed in a strange and hostile country, they were homesick and miserable, pathetically eager for a glimpse of home life and of children. It was a strange sight to see one of these great hulking troopers holding little Frances or Mary on his knee and singing her little songs of Sussex or Yorkshire, telling her tales of his own brothers and sisters and of his pleasant life before he had taken the King's cursed shilling.

They talked freely to Mr. Revere, too, revealing everything that went on in the British forces; the discontent of the common soldiers, the harshness and incompetence of the Officers. They told every plan and decision of the high command the moment it was made. All of which valuable information Mr. Revere at once passed on to the Committee of Correspondence and the Sons of Liberty.

As Sam Adams gleefully exclaimed, "Every Patriot knows what Colonel Dalrymple had for breakfast before he has digested it."

By now Mr. Revere had learned a little about riding, so every

evening after he had finished his day's work we would take short
practice rides out into the country. He was rather heavy-handed
and clumsy. He was not yet a good rider and probably never

would be a *very* good one. No such horseman, for example, as Leftenant Barnstable — who, as the saying goes, was born with a silver bit in his mouth.

But he was earnest and determined to learn, so I did all I could to teach him. For, of course, a well-trained horse, if it chooses, can do a great deal to make things more comfortable for its rider. I developed an easy rocking-chair gait, started and stopped as gently as possible, forced him to balance correctly when taking corners and hills. Soon he learned to trust in my judgment entirely and we got along very well. We made an excellent team, capable of any ordinary travel. But neither of us dreamed of the extraordinary amount of riding we were to do together.

## 7. Poor Deluded Yokels

As MR. REVERE's horsemanship improved we began taking longer rides into the country. Every few days we visited some village such as Milton, Dedham, Newton, Weston, Lexington or Concord, all on the business of the Sons of Liberty and the Committee of Correspondence.

I was horrified to see that these misguided Colonials were actually preparing for armed resistance to the King. Had it not been so serious it would have been laughable. In many of these settlements we saw the Militia drilling, and a more ridiculous sight would have been hard to imagine. Old grandfathers and young boys, well-to-do farmers and stupid yokels; all without uniforms, many without muskets, none with any idea of discipline. The common soldiers laughed and joked with their Officers (I could imagine a trooper joking with Colonel Dalrymple!) or they left in the middle of their drills to go home for supper or to visit the taverns. Their Officers were mounted on untrained farm horses, which usually shied or ran away whenever a shot was fired.

The only Militia companies showing any discipline or order at all were those which contained deserters from His Majesty's Forces. In Medford we came upon Enoch Sawtell drilling his small company, which was the best organized one we had seen yet. He came over and shook hands happily with Mr. Revere, who complimented him on the discipline of his men.

"Not much spit and polish as yet," Enoch admitted, "but you can't expect too much of that, Mr. Revere. These are free men and volunteers — and we don't use the lash." He grinned wryly. "But I'll tell you something, Mr. Revere — these men can *shoot*."

He spoke to a young lad, who ran far down the field and stood up four corncobs on a stump. Then he called four men from the ranks, lined them up and commanded, "By the numbers — LOAD." They seemed to load awkwardly, but in less than half the time that it would have taken King's soldiers. At the command FIRE three of the corncobs flipped high in the air, the fourth merely jiggled slightly. There was an outburst of jeers and cat-calls from the troop as the red-faced marksman hastily rammed home another load, dropped to one knee and fired again. This

60

time the remaining corncob exploded in small white fragments. "Would that that was Leftenant Barnstable's belt buckle," Enoch said. Then he clapped the lad on the shoulder. "Good man," he cried. "There's not a trooper in His Majesty's Forces who could do that at one third the distance."

As the proud youth returned to the ranks Mr. Revere inquired about the Minute Men.

"Twenty of them here," Enoch replied promptly. "All living within sound of the meetinghouse bell. Every man of them goes to sleep at night with musket, powder horn, bullet pouch, flint and lantern laid out beside his bed. We'll not be caught unready, I can promise you that, Mr. Revere."

Riding home, I could not but feel sorry for all these poor deluded yokels. By now I had become quite fond of Mr. Revere and his friends. To think that they were mad enough to believe that their silly Militia could seriously oppose such splendid, well-disciplined Royal Regiments as the 14th and the 29th made me very sad.

Of course they could shoot; any bumpkins who lived mostly on squirrels, rabbits, deer and wild turkeys would have to be able to shoot; but our troops were not squirrels or deer. I could just imagine Ajax's contempt. "Preposterous, my dear girl," he would snort. "One good volley and they'll scatter like rabbits."

But I did not like to think of Ajax now. . . .

It was late one evening when we got back to Boston, but late though it was there seemed to be a great bustle of excitement in the streets. As we rode into the back yard young Paul rushed out to unsaddle me.

"Father," he cried breathlessly. "The *Dartmouth* is here. She came in this afternoon, loaded with tea. Mr. Sam Adams has been looking for you. Everybody's down at Griffin's Wharf. May I go down, Father?"

"Yes," Mr. Revere answered absently, "but be careful. This means trouble." Young Paul dashed off, Mr. Revere mounted again, and we trotted down to Griffin's Wharf.

The whole town seemed to be gathered there. I could see, and hear, Sam Adams mounted on a molasses barrel making a speech. Around him were all the prominent Patriots: Dr. Warren, James Otis, Sam's cousin John Adams, Mr. Hancock. The leading members of the Sons of Liberty and the Committee of Correspondence were there as well as every well-known judge, minister, banker, lawyer and merchant. All, that is, except the Loyalists, who were noticeably absent.

As we worked our way slowly through the throng the Captain of the *Dartmouth* was arguing with Mr. Hancock. "No tea goes ashore," Mr. Hancock said firmly. "Not one ounce."

"Go back to England," the crowd roared. "Go back to England and take your rotten tea with you!"

"Listen, Mr. Hancock," the Captain pleaded, "I don't care tuppence about the blasted tea or the blasted tax or the blasted King or his blasted Ministers. I'm a good Nantucketer, I am. All I'm talking about are my ship and my crew. These men haven't been ashore for six weeks and they're getting ugly. Hang the tea, I'm sick and tired of the stuff."

After a few moments of consultation Mr. Hancock told the Captain: "Your ship will be unharmed; the Sons of Liberty guarantee its safety. As for your men, they are at perfect liberty to come ashore — but see that they bring no tea with them, not a pocketful. And the longer they stay ashore the better for all concerned."

At this announcement the crew broke into a cheer and came piling ashore, each man with a grin turning out his pockets to show that he bore none of the hated tea.

The Sons of Liberty took charge at once. Twenty-five muskets were dealt out to twenty-five men who were to act as guards, Mr. Revere one of them. The guards pushed the crowd back five paces from the ship's side and began pacing their posts as smartly as any King's sentries. The relieved Captain brought out a rocking chair and settled himself on the poop deck with his pipe and the ship's cat. Slowly the crowd melted away, leaving only a small group of the Patriot leaders and the pacing sentries. Young Paul rode me home; fed, watered and bedded me down. As he stumbled sleepily into the house all the meetinghouse bells struck three.

Mr. Revere came home a little after sunrise when the guard was changed. He slumped down wearily while Mrs. Revere, Deborah and the old lady bustled about, getting him a good hot breakfast. He had not eaten since noon of the previous day.

"Paul dear," old Mrs. Revere asked, "did you bring your mother just a little bit of that lovely English tea?"

"No, Mother, of course not. Not an ounce of that tea was unloaded or ever will be, in America."

"But I *must* have tea," the old lady wailed. "Seems to me you could have brought your poor old mother just a tiny scrap of tea."

"But Mother, you have your smuggled Dutch tea."

"Nasty old dried-up stuff," she cried, "and *so* expensive! This would be much cheaper even with the tax. I don't see why you men have to be so stubborn about a little old tax and me practically dying for a cup of really good tea."

"But Mother, I've explained and explained. It's a matter of principle, it's not the cost. England has not the right to tax us even one penny without our say-so. If we — "

At this moment the door crashed open and Sam Adams burst in. "To horse my boy, to horse," he shouted excitedly. "Word has just come that these minions of Tyranny may attempt to land the cursed Bohea at some other port. Every town on our coast must be warned. Five messengers have already left; you are the sixth. You will go to Marblehead and Salem and rouse the Sons of Liberty there. Order them to warn Gloucester, Newburyport, Portsmouth!"

"But my breakfast . . ." poor Mr. Revere protested.

"No time for breakfast, when duty calls," Sam cried. "I'll take care of that."

Young Paul had me already saddled. As Mr. Revere wearily mounted, I caught a glimpse of Sam Adams seating himself in Mr. Revere's vacant chair and contemplating with approval the steaming dishes spread before him. The last thing we heard as we headed out of the stable into a driving cold drizzle was the voice of old Mrs. Revere.

"Now surely, Mr. Adams," she was saying, "with your high position and great influence, surely you could manage to get a poor old Grandmother just a pound or so of that delicious tea?"

It was a miserable cold wet ride to Marblehead and Salem, the longest we had yet taken. In Salem I was fed and watered, while the Sons of Liberty rushed Mr. Revere off to consult with their leaders. I did hope they gave the poor man a decent meal, for he had now been twenty-four hours without food. However, I had barely finished my oats when he reappeared, mounted (with considerable groaning), and we set out on the long trip home.

As Mr. Revere stumbled wearily into the kitchen Mrs. Revere cried, "My poor Paul, do sit down and get a rest, supper will be ready in a moment. I hope they gave you a good dinner in Salem."

"Codfish," Mr. Revere answered sadly. "And Deborah, my girl, will you please fetch a pillow for my chair?" He sank onto the pillow with a groan of relief and within a few moments was enjoying his hot supper. But before he was half through his clam chowder there was a knock at the door and again Sam Adams entered. "My tea?" exclaimed old Mrs. Revere.

"Not yet, Madame," Sam answered, "but I have the matter under advisement. Come, Paul, my boy, time for changing the guard."

With another slight groan Mr. Revere rose stiffly from his half-finished meal, and donned his greatcoat; and the two set off for Griffin's Wharf.

For the next two weeks there was no peace in the Revere home, in fact in all Boston. Very soon two more tea-laden vessels, the *Eleanor* and the *Beaver,* arrived and were also moored at Griffin's Wharf. Mr. Revere was on the guard over the tea ships every night. All day he was here, there and everywhere; at meetings of the Sons of Liberty, of the Caucus Club, at mass meetings in the Old North Church, riding on business for the various committees. He had no time for his shop; when he slept I cannot imagine, and he almost never was allowed to finish a meal without interruption.

Two days after our trip to Salem his breakfast was again broken into, this time by the owner of the three tea ships, Mr.

Rotch. Mr. Rotch was a Quaker from Nantucket, dressed in dreary brown clothes. He wore his broad-brimmed hat all the time he was in the house, which struck me as being extremely ill bred, but Mr. Revere seemed used to the custom. Besides, he was far more interested in his breakfast than in Mr. Rotch. The poor shipowner was in a dreadful state of nerves and exasperation.

"Friend Revere," he begged, "surely you have some influence with these hotheads? Is there nothing you can do to make them listen to reason? Think of my poor ships, my beautiful ships!"

"Have you seen the Governor?" Mr. Revere asked.

"I have seen the Governor, I have seen the Military Commander, I have seen the Harbor Master, I have seen your Mr. Hancock, Mr. Otis, both Mr. Adamses. I have seen the Sons of Liberty and the Committee of Correspondence. None of them can, or will, do anything to help me. All they talk of are tea and taxes, taxes and tea! None of them gives a thought to me or my ships."

"Why don't you sail the tea back to England?" Mr. Revere asked, helping himself to three eggs.

"Sail, sail?" the Quaker wailed. "Would that I could! Would that I could sail to the middle of the ocean and throw the miserable trash overboard. Would that I could sail back to England and dump it on their docks. Gladly would I sail it back to China and replace it on the bushes. But sail I cannot . . ."

"Why not?" Mr. Revere asked, spearing a slice of ham.

"Because were I to attempt to sail without clearance papers the British guns on Castle William would blow my poor ships to

matchwood. And the Governor refuses me clearance papers."

" 'Tis said the Governor owns a large share in this tea venture," Mr. Revere observed. "But why not leave matters as they are? Your ships are guarded from all harm, nothing will happen to them."

"Because of the port regulations, friend Revere. Surely you are aware that any ship docking in Boston Harbor must be unloaded within twenty days, else ship and cargo will be seized by the authorities? I cannot go and I cannot stay . . . and the twentieth day is rapidly approaching." He began pacing the floor frantically.

Mr. Revere, having finished his breakfast, also rose. "I regret, friend Rotch," he said firmly, "that I can do nothing to assist you. I can only assure you that your ships will remain untouched. But bear this in mind: Not one pound of that tea will be unloaded in Boston by you or anyone else, while it still carries a tax. As long as that tax remains, your ships will stay right where they are until, if necessary, they grow barnacles two feet thick."

"Tea and taxes, taxes and tea!" the Quaker shouted, snatching up his coat and rushing forth. "I am sickened to death of the words."

"Did I hear someone say *tea?*" old Mrs. Revere called from upstairs. "Is that Mr. Adams with my pound of tea?"

## 8.  Big Doings at Griffin's Wharf

December sixteenth, the decisive day, had now arrived. On the morrow the twenty days of grace would end. Then something *must* happen. The ships would either have to sail or be unloaded. But the authorities stood firm

71

on their decree that they should not sail, and twenty-five armed, determined guards on Griffin's Wharf said they should not be unloaded. So did the thousands who milled about the streets all through that day.

At the Old South Church there was a great mass meeting. Five to seven thousand persons jammed the church or stood in the streets nearby. There were also two smaller meetings of equal importance. In a back room of the *Boston Globe's* printing house were gathered most of Boston's greatest merchants. At the Green Dragon Tavern the rough-and-ready Sons of Liberty held forth. Mr. Revere tried to attend all three meetings and kept me busy the whole day galloping from one to the other.

Then late in the afternoon the distracted Mr. Rotch drove out to Milton to make one last despairing plea to the Governor for clearance papers. Of course Mr. Revere and I accompanied him, for everything depended on the Governor's answer.

When the poor Quaker emerged from the Governor's Mansion it was clear that his trip had been useless. His face was pale and drawn, his shoulders sagged. As he climbed into his chaise Mr. Revere called, "No papers?"

"No papers," Mr. Rotch answered with a gesture of despair.

At once we started back to Boston at a breakneck gallop. In town the streets were almost deserted; everyone was still at the mass meeting or at Griffin's Wharf. To a lookout at the Green Dragon Mr. Revere shouted, "No papers," and repeated the same cry as we passed the *Boston Globe* office. Then we made for the Old South Church.

The sun had set and it was growing dark now, but the throng, recognizing Mr. Revere and me, cleared a way to the door. There he dismounted and I could see him making his way slowly through the packed aisles. Reaching the rostrum he whispered something in Sam Adams's ear, then returned and remounted. Sam Adams went on with his speech, his voice now quite hoarse, for he had been orating most of the day.

There was nothing to do now but await the arrival of Mr. Rotch. It was an uncomfortable wait, for the night was cold, but the crowd did not seem to mind. They were too heated with excitement to feel the weather.

As Mr. Rotch's chaise came clopping up, the silent crowd parted and gave him passage. He made his slow way to the rostrum and joined Sam Adams and the other speakers. Through the open door we could see him face the audience, and although it was impossible to hear his words it was clear from his distraught manner and hopeless gestures what his message was.

Suddenly Sam Adams burst out in a booming voice that filled the church and echoed over the heads of the tense throng: "This meeting can do nothing more to save the country!"

Clearly this was an arranged signal, for no sooner had he spoken than Mr. Revere clapped heels to my ribs and we raced for the Revere house. Like a dark river the crowd from the mass meeting began to flow down the streets leading to the wharves.

While young Paul fed and watered me I was watching an odd sight in the kitchen. Spread out on the table was a strange collection of clothes, evidently old garments turned inside out and decorated here and there with feathers and bits of red cloth. There was an old knitted cap, also stuck full of feathers. While

the children, dancing with excitement, looked on, Mr. Revere
hastily smeared his face with grease and then with soot. He
added a few stripes of red and yellow paint, slipped on the weird
garments and the headdress and snatched up a hatchet.

"Daddy is an Indian, Daddy is an Indian!" the children
shrieked in glee.

"How do I look?" Mr. Revere asked his wife a bit sheepishly.

"Silly," she replied frankly and kissed him good-by, getting
well smeared with soot in the process.

"And please, Paul, don't forget my tea," old Mrs. Revere called after him.

We emerged on North Street just as a large band of men, similarly attired, was passing. They greeted Mr. Revere with subdued grunts as he placed himself at their head. It was amazing how quiet the crowds were. All day they had been arguing, cheering and shouting; now there was not a sound save the shuffle of thousands of feet and the clicking of my shoes on the cobbles.

There was a huge and constantly growing throng on the wharf, but they opened up to allow our band to pass. Evidently everything had been carefully planned, for our Indians now divided into three bands, one for each ship. Mr. Revere led the *Dartmouth* contingent, having placed me in care of young Paul.

As the Indians swarmed aboard, the captains and their mates made no protest but stood about the decks smoking their pipes and watching the proceedings with only a mild interest. The hatches were quickly removed, several men went below, and in a few moments the tea chests began to come up in a steady stream. To avoid unnecessary noise the chests were passed from hand to hand with the greatest care, the lids soundlessly pried off and the hated contents poured over the rail.

Two of His Majesty's armed ships were anchored not far off. I felt sure that at any moment they would come alive and perhaps pour a volley of grapeshot into the toiling Mohawks or the packed crowd. But the ships remained dark and silent.

"Officers all drunk, or playing cards," a nearby sailor grunted. "Crew asleep, including the watch."

I also feared that we might suddenly hear the roll of drums and see the advancing columns of Royal troops, but all was quiet in the town and a returning spy reported that Castle William was wrapped in slumber.

Through most of the night the Indians toiled and grunted. The Harbor waters became covered with a thick scum of sodden tea leaves. Here and there little islands of dry tea floated for a while before slowly sinking into the brine. I could not help thinking how the sight would have distressed the elder Mrs. Revere. The eastern sky was growing pale when the last chest was emptied, the hatches replaced and the decks swept clean.

Despite the cold night Mr. Revere was sweating profusely, as

were all the rest of the masqueraders. He mounted wearily and prepared to depart. At that moment Mr. Rotch, still pale and harassed, joined the group.

"Well, friend Rotch," Mr. Revere laughed, "your ships at last are unloaded — and unscratched. There seems no reason why you cannot sail at your pleasure, unless the old turkey gobbler in Castle William can concoct one."

"I do not know who thee be, in that heathen garb," the Quaker replied, "but I thank thee one and all for thy kind consideration. Never before have I beheld such genteelly behaved savages." He almost managed a smile.

At home Mr. Revere hastened to remove his outlandish costume and wash most of the soot from his face. The old lady snatched up the discarded garments and hastened upstairs with them, while Mrs. Revere and Deborah set out a large and steaming breakfast.

"We were dreadfully worried," Mrs. Revere said. "Did everything go as planned?"

"Exactly," Mr. Revere exulted. "Three hundred and forty cases of choice Bohea are now steeping in the waters of our fair Harbor. It was a stupendous Tea Party. An expensive one, too, for His Majesty and the East India Company. I understand that the refreshments cost about eighteen thousand pounds sterling, but of course there were a *great* many guests."

In high good humor he attacked his breakfast, but had barely begun when there came the usual knock at the door. In stepped Sam Adams, several members of the Committee and a great many of the neighbors.

Sam Adams mounted a footstool. "Paul Revere, Patriot and Citizen," he declaimed, still a bit hoarse from yesterday's marathon of talk, "it is our high privilege to confer a great honor upon you. The news of last night's glorious happenings must at once be conveyed to our brother Patriots in the great city of New York. Many have sought the privilege, but the unanimous choice of the Committee has fallen upon you, my friend."

"It *is* a great honor," Mr. Revere agreed, a bit ruefully. "But it is near four hundred and fifty miles there and back, and it's midwinter — and I haven't had my breakfast."

"No time for breakfast when duty . . ." Adams began, eying the steaming dishes hungrily.

"There *is* time for breakfast, Sam Adams, for *him*," Mrs. Revere interrupted. "Besides I have his saddlebags to pack and dear

78

Sherry hasn't half finished her oats. Now just you sit down and cool your heels and let the poor man eat his breakfast in peace. Perhaps I'll give you a cup of coffee — later." She flounced upstairs with some remark about people who were getting "too big for their breeches," which I did not understand, but which seemed to quiet Mr. Adams and the Committee very effectively.

Eventually Mr. Revere finished his breakfast and I mine. Mrs. Revere came down, bringing the packed saddlebags, which young Paul quickly strapped to the saddle. Mr. Revere kissed his wife and all the children and was ready to depart.

Just then old Mrs. Revere came running down, fairly skipping with joy. She held a teacup half filled with something.

"See what I have," she cried. "Just look! Real English tea, the finest Bohea, a half-teacupful! *Won't* Rachel and Debby and I have a tea party this afternoon!"

"But Mother," Mr. Revere exclaimed, "where on earth — how — ?"

"Out of your silly Indian costume," she laughed gleefully. "Out of the creases and the torn lining and the headdress. You men *will* play Indian. There's some more, too, but I'm saving that for Mr. Sam Adams. *It* came out of your shoes."

## 9.  Revere Rides Again — and Again

THAT TRIP to New York was one
which I shall never forget. I feel sure that Mr. Revere will not
either. While he had learned to ride fairly well, he had never

ridden any great distance. In fact he had hardly ever been out of sight of Beacon Hill. New York was over two hundred miles away; neither of us knew the route; and, as Mr. Revere had said, it was midwinter. It was snowing slightly as we crossed Boston Neck and headed west and south.

We rode hard all that day. As we passed through each village Mr. Revere shouted out the news of the great Tea Party. Everywhere it was received with the greatest excitement, the villagers crowding about, urging Mr. Revere to tarry, to rest and eat. But he refused to waste a moment, merely inquiring about the route and dashing on to the next town.

By nightfall we had covered about forty-five miles. I was well tired, and poor Mr. Revere was so sore and exhausted that he could scarcely dismount. Our host for the night was the head of the Sons of Liberty and the leading citizen of the village. I was given the best of attention, well rubbed down, well fed and watered.

As soon as Mr. Revere had announced his news the Sons of Liberty gathered on the village green, celebrating with bonfires and musketry. Before the rejoicings were well started, however, the lights in our host's house were all extinguished and I was sure that Mr. Revere was being allowed to sleep soundly. Goodness knows he deserved it.

We were off at sunrise and the next day was a repetition of the first. In fact each day was like another: riding posthaste from dawn to sunset, being fed, sleeping — and then off again with the rising sun. I lost all track of time, I had no idea of where we were or even what Colony we were in.

The road, proudly called the King's Highway, of course was miserable, like all Colonial roads. It was filled with bogholes, ruts, rocks and occasional tree stumps. In England it would have been scarcely called a road. It was the roughest sort of going and I shall never understand how Mr. Revere stood it. As for me, I was in excellent condition and never ceased to be thankful to the kindly farrier for the splendid manner in which he had shod me.

All through this long journey I continually wondered at the enthusiasm of these poor deluded peasants. As we got farther and farther from Boston and the King's troops, the rebellious temper of the people was more and more openly displayed. Every village had its Liberty Pole, the Militia drilled on every green, military supplies were stored unguarded in almost every meetinghouse. The people could not do enough for Mr. Revere and me. Even the inhabitants of Connecticut, noted for their surliness and sharp dealings, were kind and helpful — moderately.

I was beginning to feel that this strange and savage country had no end when suddenly, on the afternoon of the fifth day, we found ourselves on the banks of the Harlem River. A ferry took us across its treacherous tides, we were guided to the Bourie

Lane and I put my last energy into a steady gallop down its smooth broad surface. We passed southward through a stretch of pleasant rolling farms with the smoking chimneys of New York City growing ever closer. They were a most welcome sight to both of us.

Arrived in the city we were directed to the home of Mr. John Lamb, who headed the rebellious elements in New York. I was at once stabled, rubbed down and well fed, while Mr. Lamb took charge of Mr. Revere. I fell asleep at once, but all through the night was wakened now and then by the sounds of joyful celebration. I could see the glow of bonfires and hear cheers, shouts and the discharges of musketry.

As usual Mr. Revere appeared at sunrise, accompanied by Mr. Lamb.

"But, Mr. Revere," the latter was arguing, "this is so unreasonable! Surely you must stay a day or so to rest yourself and your horse. The poor thing is thoroughly exhausted, you are too. Five days from Boston is remarkable speed at any time; in this weather it is miraculous. What is more, we want you to see our city, meet our prominent leaders and talk to the gentlemen of the press. After all, your mission is accomplished; why such haste to get back to Boston?"

"There is much that I can do in Boston," Mr. Revere answered. "Our poor city is still under the heel of the redcoats." Then he smiled. "Also, I have a large family, Mr. Lamb. I hope to spend at least a part of Christmas with them."

"Christmas?" Mr. Lamb exclaimed. "But that is quite impossible! Today is the twenty-second; you cannot think to make the trip in three days and a half!"

"Perhaps not," Mr. Revere laughed, and slapped me on the neck, "but we can try, can't we, Sherry?"

However, he did allow himself to be persuaded to stay for a late breakfast to meet many of the leading Patriots of New York. I thoroughly relished the few hours of extra rest. It was almost noon before we were able to get away, so we only progressed as far as the village of New Rochelle by nightfall.

We made all possible speed the next day and the next, but the weather was against us. Deep snow and a biting northeast wind so delayed us that by Christmas Eve we had only reached New London in the Connecticut Colony.

It was pleasant to see the busy shoppers in the streets, all laden with Christmas gifts, the candlelighted houses, the gay green of Christmas trees, holly and mistletoe. It was pleasant, but sad for us, for Boston and home were still three days' journey

84

away. I must admit that I was almost as disappointed as my master, for I found myself longing for my snug little stable, for the warmth of the kitchen and the happy chatter of the Revere children.

Our host here was a wealthy shipowner. At sunrise he accompanied Mr. Revere to the stable, arguing, as had Mr. Lamb, that we tarry at least through Christmas, but Mr. Revere was determined to push on. "Our Boston Committee is most anxious to hear how the news was received in New York," he said. "I must hurry along as fast as possible. Also, I fear for my family. Almost anything might happen now in Boston at any moment."

As he was about to mount, the shipowner's wife hurried out, accompanied by a servant who carried a rather large pack. "I am taking the liberty of sending a few little things for your dear family's Christmas, Mr. Revere," she said, "although they may be a trifle late."

The pack contained four beautiful French dolls, one for each of the younger children, for Miss Deborah a lovely shawl from India, and for Mrs. Revere a Chinese brooch of gold and ivory. Not to be outdone, our host produced a small package. "For your honored mother," he laughed. "The best Oolong tea, smuggled in on one of my ships. She may drink it with a clear conscience, for it has paid no tax." For young Paul he had a beautiful little English flintlock pistol, its butt all inlaid with silver. "As for you, sir," he continued — "with my admiring respect . . ." and handed Mr. Revere a handsome cap, made of the richest sea otter fur. Mr. Revere donned it at once, his old hat and the pack of gifts were strapped on over the saddlebags, and amid profuse thanks and cries of "Merry Christmas!" and "Good luck!" we were again on our way.

We reached home on the evening of the twenty-seventh, two days after Christmas. How thrilling it was to see the lights of the Revere kitchen! I had not realized how homesick I had been, how deeply I had missed what I now considered "my family." Our welcome was tumultuous: hugs, kisses, questions, even a tear or two of relief. I almost shed a few myself on discovering that my stable had been all hung with Christmas greens and decorated with carrots, shiny red apples and colorful ears of Indian corn.

Young Paul hastened to rub me down, bring me a large pan of steaming mash and a generous measure of grain. As I munched my supper contentedly I could see Mr. Revere equally enjoying his.

A small Christmas tree occupied one corner of the kitchen, under it many small gifts still unwrapped.

"*Now* we can have our Christmas," Miss Deborah cried happily as Mr. Revere finished the last of his supper. The other children pounced on their presents with shrieks of joy; when the shipowner's pack was opened the excitement became riotous. Old Mrs. Revere was speechless with happiness over her tea.

"The children were *so* good about waiting for you," Mrs. Revere said to her husband. "They said they would delay Christmas until you and Sherry came home, if they had to wait until spring. And now tell me all about New York. Is it as grand and exciting as 'tis said?"

Mr. Revere, relaxing with his pipe, a pillow in his chair and

86

his feet in comfortable slippers, smiled at his wife. "I hardly know," he said. "All I saw of New York was Mr. Lamb's guest room and his dining room."

He had just begun to describe his trip when there arrived Sam Adams, Dr. Warren, Mr. Otis and Mr. Hancock from the Committee. Mr. Revere told them of the great enthusiasm in New York and in all the towns along the way. He gave them a letter from the Sons of Liberty of New York, which Dr. Warren at once read.

"Splendid!" he cried. "Governor Tryon has sent the New York tea ships back to England with their tea still aboard. The Sons of Liberty promise us their full support and co-operation. You have accomplished a difficult mission in noble fashion, Mr. Revere. The cause of Liberty is deeply indebted to you."

"That it is, Paul my boy, that it is," Sam Adams broke in. "And now for Griffin's Wharf. Time to change the guard."

"Guard?" Mr. Revere asked in dismay. "Are the tea ships still there?"

"Indeed yes," Mr. Hancock answered. "The lobster-backs have trumped up some excuse for detaining them. Poor Mr. Rotch is well-nigh distracted, but the Sons of Liberty have guaranteed their safety, so the guard must be continued."

With a slight groan Mr. Revere rose from his comfortable cushion, donned his boots, fur cap and greatcoat and tramped off with Sam Adams.

Next morning while he ate his breakfast and the family still admired their Christmas gifts Mr. Revere told the whole story of our trip, never ceasing to praise my part in it. "Now," he concluded, with a vast yawn, "I think I shall sleep the rest of the day."

But he had scarcely spoken when all the meetinghouse bells began to ring; drums beat; there were shouts, cheers and the firing of muskets. The people of Boston were celebrating the good news from New York. All day the kitchen was filled with Sons of Liberty come to congratulate Mr. Revere on the success of his difficult trip. Needless to say I came in for considerable attention too, and I must say that it gave me far more satisfaction than had winning any number of races for my former master.

One of the visitors was the good farrier. He inspected my shoes and hoofs carefully, felt me all over and trotted me around the yard looking for any signs of lameness. "Sound as a dollar, fit as a fiddle," he cried. "I told you she was a fine horse, Mr. Revere; don't know's I've ever seen a better. Hard to believe she was ever that poor scarecrow of Stinky Nat's."

Now for a few months we had a period of comparative peace in the Revere household. Of course Mr. Revere continued to attend his meetings and we had to make many short rides into the surrounding country, but he did find time to do considerable work in his shop. This was fortunate, for his trade had been sorely neglected and money had become scarce in the home. Indeed had it not been for the many donations of food from the grateful deserters I hardly know how we would have gotten along.

This however, was but the calm before the storm.

On May tenth a fast ship arrived from England bearing dire tidings. His Majesty, furious over the destruction of the tea, was determined to teach these rebellious Colonials a lesson they never would forget. He and his Ministers had passed several harsh laws, one of which ordered the Port of Boston closed to all ships. General Gage with four thousand fresh troops and considerable artillery would arrive shortly to enforce these new laws. Governor Hutchinson, considered too easy-going, was leaving for England and General Gage would now be Governor as well as Commander of all Royal Forces.

I did not realize how grave a threat this closing of the Port was until I heard Dr. Warren talking it over with Mr. Revere. "It is not only a calamity to our trade," the good Doctor said, "it means ruin, starvation and death to our people. Practically all our business is based on shipping, most of our food comes by boat. Our shipyards will have to close, our ships will rot at their wharves, all our banks and business firms will fail. Men, women and children will die of hunger and want. It is a form of slow murder. We must appeal to our sister Colonies for assistance."

Sam Adams and the other leaders were already busy. A plea for aid was drafted, and Mr. Revere and I were chosen to carry it to the other Colonies.

This trip, the longest we had yet made, took us all the way to Philadelphia in the Pennsylvania Colony. There, while we slept, a great mass meeting pledged the aid and support of all the other Colonies to our poor threatened Boston. Even the wealthy planters of the far-off Carolinas promised shiploads of rice, and the great General Washington announced that if need arose he would himself raise a thousand men and march them to the relief of our city.

We were back home on the twenty-eighth of May, having accomplished this long journey in the remarkably short time of two weeks. Of course, there was the usual ringing of bells in celebration of the promising news we brought — but underneath there was deep foreboding, for in just three days the Port would be closed. What would happen then none could tell.

All during our ride through New Jersey, so beautiful in its blossoms, so peaceful and far from threats of war and privation, my thoughts had all been with my dear Revere children. What would happen to *them* when this cruel law was enforced? I thought of the bitter Boston winters; what would they be like without sufficient food or fuel?

Doubtless the rebels had been wrong in destroying the tea, but did that excuse destroying a whole city? Of course they had flouted His Majesty's authority, but was this a kingly way to avenge a slight — by starving children and old people? I could picture them all: old Mrs. Revere, Deborah, Paul, Sarah, Frances, little Mary and Elizabeth, shivering in their half-heated home, wasting away of hunger, while the fat, warmly clad, overfed soldiers of the King strutted it through the deserted streets.

For the first time in my life I began to have doubts as to the divine wisdom of the King and his advisers. The glory of his Armed Forces, its Officers and Gentlemen, began to seem shoddy and tarnished.

RL

## 10.  Closed Port

D URING OUR ABSENCE General Gage
had arrived with his fresh troops and the town now fairly
crawled with red-coated soldiers, about one to every four
civilians.

"What sort of man is this General Gage?" Mr. Revere asked
one of the homesick Britishers who frequented our kitchen.

"Puffed-up old fuss-budget," the trooper replied. "Never does
nothink, never will. 'Is orders is to arrest all the rebel ring-
leaders: you, Dr. Warren, Mr. Hancock, Mr. Otis and the rest.

What does 'e do? Nothink, that's what. Don't worry." He laughed and tweaked little Mary's pigtails. "Ever 'e makes up 'is mind you'll know about it in plenty time to be in Philadelphy 'fore 'e moves."

The dreaded June first arrived; the Port was closed to all ships. As Dr. Warren had prophesied, the shipyards shut down, grass grew on the wharves, countinghouses and banks closed or failed, the shelves of the merchants grew bare. However, no one went hungry — yet. For none of the other ports was closed and there were half a dozen within easy distance of Boston where ships could unload and have their cargoes freighted into the city by wagon.

And from the surrounding country the farmers drove in herds of cattle and flocks of sheep. Ducks, geese, chickens and turkeys were plentiful and, of course, quantities of fish. There were even great piles of firewood stored up against the coming winter. Often we saw Enoch Sawtell shepherding a flock of sheep under the very noses of his former comrades. General Putnam — "Old Put," as he was affectionately called — arrived from distant Connecticut, ostensibly driving a flock of sheep, but in reality spying out the lay of the land and the disposition of the Royal troops.

So the hot summer of '74 dragged along, with General Gage doing nothing, while the Patriots busily gathered together military stores. Mr. Revere worked in his shop whenever he was able, but most of his time now was devoted to carrying messages to the outlying towns and to perfecting his spy system.

Great numbers of the Sons of Liberty being idle, they devoted their time to spying on the British. What with their coming in to report and troopers who came to visit and also to supply news, the Revere kitchen became a perfect information center. Mr. Revere was kept busy gathering, sorting and passing on all these reports to Dr. Warren, Sam Adams and the other leaders.

Then, in September, a Congress of all the Colonies was called to meet in Philadelphia. Sam Adams and his cousin John were chosen to represent the Massachusetts Colony.

There was some difficulty about Sam Adams's clothes, for, the man having devoted all his time to the cause of Liberty and none to making a living, his appearance was extremely threadbare, hardly a credit to the proud Colony of Massachusetts. However, various more fortunate Patriots donated new, or almost new, garments; so he departed for Philadelphia in high good spirits and possessed of a very creditable wardrobe.

The Congress convened on September fifth and on the

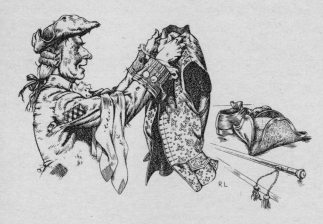

eleventh we again set off for Philadelphia. This was in connection with some very rebellious set of resolutions called the "Suffolk Resolves," which I did not understand at all, but which they seemed to consider of great importance.

In Philadelphia Sam Adams greeted Mr. Revere affectionately, but it was clear that his manner was somewhat subdued. Mr. John Adams explained this to Mr. Revere later. "There are so many Delegates here," he said with a smile, "who can talk faster and louder and longer than poor Sam that it has rather crushed his spirit, but he will soon rebound, never fear."

All the great men of the Colonies were gathered for the Congress. We saw the famous Dr. Franklin, who had come from Boston originally. He was short and dumpy in figure and dressed somewhat like a Quaker. He did not impress me especially.

General George Washington, on the other hand, was tremendously impressive. A splendid tall man, beautifully uniformed, he looked every inch a great soldier and leader. Mr. Revere was introduced to him by Mr. John Adams. The General spoke to him most graciously, commending him for the splendid riding he had done in the Patriot cause and for his valued service in reporting on the British troops in Boston. He even spoke admiringly of me, looking me over with much interest, for he was a great lover of horses.

He seemed to talk with some difficulty, however, frequently grasping his jaw and finally bursting out with, "Confound these dratted teeth."

"General," Mr. Adams suggested, "in addition to his other talents Mr. Revere is a well-known artist in teeth. I am sure he

would be delighted to do what he can to alleviate your trouble."

The General at once snatched out the offending set, which even to my inexpert eye seemed to be quite crudely made, and handed them to Mr. Revere. The latter sadly shook his head while carefully inspecting them. "If I only had the proper tools . . ." he said regretfully. But he took out his jackknife, whittled, scraped and pried for a few moments, then handed them back to the General.

General Washington replaced them, clicked his jaws once or twice — and a happy smile wreathed his usually stern countenance. "Wonderful!" he exclaimed. "Quite miraculous. Immeasurably more comfortable! My dear sir, I thank you from the bottom of my heart, or perhaps I should say — my gums." Still smiling, he held out his hand, "I have often heard of Yankee ingenuity, sir, but this far transcends mere ingenuity. It is sheer genius, in its purest form."

"I thank you, sir," Mr. Revere replied modestly. "If you are ever in the vicinity of Boston I should consider it an honor to fit you with a really worthy set. At no cost, naturally, and guaranteed for life." He handed the General one of his engraved cards, and in a happy frame of mind we set forth on our homeward journey.

Scarcely were we settled at home before we were again off for Philadelphia with important letters to the Adams cousins from Dr. Warren. We now knew the route so well that Mr. Revere could often take long naps while he rode, and Mr. Lamb in New York laughingly took to calling his home "The Courier's Rest."

This time Mr. Revere took along a small kit of dental tools and, I understood, gave General Washington's teeth a thorough renovation which was deeply appreciated. The General presented him with a handsome pair of horse-pistols and saddle holsters. They gave us a rather military air, but Mr. Revere had to admit that he hadn't the slightest idea of how to shoot them.

Then, in December, two events of importance occurred. The first was the arrival of a new little Revere, a boy, who was promptly named Joshua — a rather homely name, *I* thought. The second was our trip to Portsmouth, New Hampshire, the most rigorous one we ever made.

General Gage, his ears burning with reprimands from home, was at last stung into taking some action. In Fort William and Mary, near Portsmouth, New Hampshire, lay a large supply of Royal powder and small arms guarded by only five troopers and a Captain. About mid-December it dawned on the General that perhaps these supplies ought to be removed to a safer place. He would send a secret expedition to accomplish this — very secret indeed. . . . Scarcely had he finished giving the necessary instructions to his Officers before a spy was knocking on our kitchen door with the news.

In a matter of moments, Mr. Revere was up, dressed and in the saddle. After a short pause at Dr. Warren's, we set out for Durham and Portsmouth. It was one of the coldest nights I have ever experienced, the temperature well below zero. There was an icy northeast wind and it was snowing lightly.

The roads in this section were abominable at best; tonight they were unspeakable. The puddles were all turned to ice, the ruts were frozen hard as flint. It was impossible to make any speed, yet speed was imperative. Mr. Revere wisely made no attempt to guide me. He dropped the reins over the pommel, rolled his hands in his cape and gave me my head. I could imagine how grateful he was for the new fur cap, which, pulled down tightly, covered his ears and cheeks. Now and then he would dismount and run along beside me to restore his circulation.

The sun rose, a cold hazy sun, which did little to warm us,

and still we rode. Now that it was light I left the road whenever possible and took to the open fields where the going was slightly better. The distance was only about fifty miles, we should have covered it by now, but we were barely halfway there. About noon we stopped at a lonely farmhouse where I was watered and fed while Mr. Revere thawed out by the kitchen fire and snatched a bite to eat. Then we pushed on.

It was long past dark when I stumbled up to General Sullivan's home in Durham. So stiff and cold was Mr. Revere that he had to be helped to dismount. General Sullivan at once roused the Militia and urged Mr. Revere to pause and rest, but he would not hear of it. Under the light of a clear moon we hastened on to Portsmouth.

Here the Minute Men and the Militia sprang to arms, boats were manned and some four hundred Patriots dropped quietly down the river toward Fort William and Mary. Not until the last boat had disappeared around a bend in the river would Mr. Revere consent to eat a good hot meal and go to bed.

Just at sunrise we were awakened from our exhausted slumbers by the jubilant return of the expedition. The British Captain Cochran and his five men had fired one volley, which had harmed no one, then surrendered the fort. The fuming Captain was tied up, while the Militia broke open the magazine and removed the stores. In the boats were one hundred casks of powder, worth more than gold to the Colonials, as well as one hundred muskets and pistols. With cheers and much jollity these invaluable supplies were loaded in oxcarts and started off to Durham.

Just before they left, however, a scout came paddling upriver at top speed. He reported that less than an hour after the expedition's departure from the fort there had arrived from Boston His Majesty's frigate *Scarborough* and a large sloop bearing several companies of Royal soldiers. General Gage's very secret expedition was just one hour too late! As the people realized how narrowly they had missed losing this great prize, Mr. Revere and I were hailed as heroes for our timely warning.

We started back for Boston at once. Mr. Revere was always anxious about his family. And although the weather was still bitter, there was now no need for such great haste; we made frequent stops for food and rest, spent the night at a comfortable inn, and reached home at noon the next day.

Dr. Warren and the other leaders were elated; the good news spread like wildfire. Meetinghouse bells rang and all day the kitchen was thronged with rejoicing Sons of Liberty, the confusion livened now and then by a triumphant crow from the very young Joshua. A British spy reported that General Gage had narrowly escaped a stroke of apoplexy.

Although we were not yet in dire need of food, things were becoming somewhat meager. The great ranks of firewood and the large haystack which had almost filled the back yard were now sadly depleted; only a sack or two of my grain remained. Lines of care were beginning to mark Mrs. Revere's pleasant face. Mr. Revere's business was at a standstill. No one visited the shop — save an occasional British Officer to order some trinket which usually was not paid for. The long hard winter was beginning to tell on everyone.

For some time now Mr. Revere had been contemplating moving his family outside the city, where food and fuel were more plentiful. Now there occurred an incident which settled the matter for him and left no choice.

We were riding quietly down Milk Street one day when we came upon a mounted British Officer speaking to a Sergeant and two privates. Such a sight was not at all uncommon, but to my alarm I recognized the Officer as Leftenant Sir Cedric Barn-stable and the horse, of course, as Ajax! Involuntarily I tried to turn into a side street, but Mr. Revere impatiently twitched the reins and rode directly toward the group. To him they were just another group of British soldiers.

As we approached I could see the Leftenant's pale blue eyes fixed uncertainly on me; then as we were about to pass he wheeled Ajax around, barring our progress.

"Tha-tha-tha-that's a very fi-fi-fi-fine mare fo-fo-for a country bu-bu-bu-bu-bumpkin t-to-to-to be riding," he drawled arro-gantly. "Whe-whe-whe-where d-d-d-di-did yu-yu-you stee-stee-steal her?"

"She was not stolen," Mr. Revere answered calmly.

"Say *sir* when you speak to your betters," the Sergeant growled.

Mr. Revere remained silent.

Ajax glared at me contemptuously. "Deserter!" he snorted. "Traitor! Spy!"

Mr. Revere attempted to pass on, but the Leftenant, half drawing his sword, shouted angrily, "Sta-sta-sta-stop him." The Sergeant snatched my bridle roughly, the two privates fiddled with their muskets.

At the Sergeant's heavy grasp on my bridle, the smell of stale beer on his breath, his coarse bloodshot face so close to mine, a sudden madness seized me.

Until that moment I had not fully realized how glorious it was to be free! Free of the everlasting monotony of barracks life, the deadly round of parade and drill, drill and parade . . .

free of the brutal grooms, callous Officers, stupid overfed stable-
mates — like Ajax!

In a great blinding flash I knew that I would die rather than
exchange my new-found liberty for that old prisonlike existence
I had once thought so glorious. I was a free horse! I was a Colonial! I was a Patriot, my life dedicated to the ideals of Liberty
and Freedom!

With a scream I reared, slashing wickedly at the terrified
Sergeant. I wheeled, gave Ajax a vicious kick on the hock and
sped down the street.

Fortunately Mr. Revere had not been unseated; now he
gathered up the reins and urged me to still greater speed. Behind us we heard shouts and the heavy thunder of Ajax's hoofs.
There was the crash of a pistol shot and I felt the burn of a
bullet that just creased my hip.

We whirled into a side street, then up a narrow alley. Ajax
was fat and bloated from lack of exercise; I was lean, my
muscles like whipcord. On the open road I could have outdistanced him with ease, but the narrow twisting streets and blind
corners gave little opportunity for real speed.

Suddenly from the stench I realized that we were passing the
rear of Nat Sime's glue factory. I caught a glimpse of Hezekiah
seated on an upturned barrel enjoying his morning pipe. He
recognized us and, looking back, saw the pursuing Officer. For
one of his sluggish mind he acted with amazing promptness.
With almost one motion he sprang up, flipped the barrel into
the middle of the lane and disappeared into the fastness of the
factory.

The Leftenant reined in, Ajax slithered to a stop and crashed into the barrel, not hard enough to cause a fall but enough to cause them considerable delay. As we rounded the next corner I heard the roar of the Leftenant's other pistol, but this time the bullet went wild. Mr. Revere knew these streets and alleys as well as he knew the palm of his hand; and in a short time, by doubling and twisting, we were safe from pursuit.

But it was clear now that Boston, in daylight, was no longer safe for either him or me. We were becoming too well known, and now this open defiance of one of His Majesty's Officers would add greatly to our danger. Without pause Mr. Revere headed for Boston Neck, the only way out of the city.

General Gage had bestirred himself sufficiently to fortify the Neck and establish a guard there. Luckily the sentry on duty was one of the soldiers who frequented the Revere kitchen. He gave no sign of recognition but merely waved us on without search or question.

Safely out of Boston we proceeded at a leisurely jogtrot

through Cambridge and eventually to Charlestown, just across the river from Boston's North End. Here Mr. Revere found Colonel Conant, to whom he explained his desire to move his family out of Boston. The good Colonel and various other Sons of Liberty soon found a suitable house with a comfortable stable for me. After dark, leaving me bedded down, Mr. Revere borrowed a boat and rowed across to Boston to spend the night with his family.

The events of that day had left me strangely exhilarated in mind; sleep was slow in coming. The realization that I had completely cast off my allegiance to the Crown and thrown in my lot with these rebellious Colonists should have deeply shocked a horse of my traditions and upbringing, but it did not. On the contrary, I felt a wonderful sense of uplift and freedom; as though I had been born again into a new life in a fresh new world.

Across the water the tall spire of the Old North Church rose clean and sharp in the moonlight. I thought of my old army life. At this hour I would have been stabled with a dozen or two other horses, stamping, shifting and grumbling. Outside, the endless heavy pacing of sentries. Nothing to look forward to, save the morning drumbeat rousing us out; the same rough currying, the same gruff commands, the same sullen obedience, the same daily parade, the same unvaried food, the same dreadful monotony.

But now! The morrow was something to be looked forward to with joyful anticipation. Tomorrow I would doubtless be reunited with my laughing, affectionate family. Tomorrow we might take to the open road, Mr. Revere and I. Where? Anywhere — New York, Philadelphia, New Hampshire, Rhode Island, Connecticut. New scenes, new faces, new experiences.

"Your master is your master," Ajax had once stupidly said. All very well that, for a dull-minded King's horse, but not for a free and independent Colonial. Mr. Revere was no master — he was my friend, my loved and respected friend. We were not master and slave, we were partners, partners in a great new and shining adventure.

Across the still waters Old North's bell tolled out the hour of midnight as I fell into a sound and untroubled sleep.

106

## 11. Lights in the Belfry

Now MR. REVERE began the slow and difficult task of removing his family to Charlestown. One or two at a time the older children were rowed across, usually at night. Beds, bedding and other necessities came by oxcart across the Neck. Of course the Neck and the Charlestown ferry were both guarded by British troops,but since most of the sentries knew the family and their kitchen well they always managed to look the other way when any Revere or Revere belongings came along.

Last to arrive were Mrs. Revere, young Joshua and the old lady, carefully clutching the last remnants of her pound of tea.

By the end of a week we were all settled, most comfortably and happily.

After the confinement and gloom of the city the change to the country was enjoyed by everyone. It did my heart good to see how quickly the children shook off their city pallor and became rosy and active again. My new stable did not open into the kitchen, which I regretted slightly, but since I had the freedom of the premises I did not miss anything that went on.

With great labor Mr. Revere managed to bring over his engraving equipment and press. This was set up in a shed next to my stable and here he busied himself all day, engraving and printing various things for Congress and the Army — chiefly money. The money was not worth much compared to British gold, but that was no fault of Mr. Revere's. He did his part well and everyone agreed the money looked very pretty. Almost every evening, as soon as it became dark, he rowed across to Boston to the old home, where he could keep in touch with his spies and visit with young Paul, who had stayed behind to watch over the house and shop. From these visits Mr. Revere always brought home much interesting news.

With the coming of spring and the arrival of wrathful letters from London, General Gage had begun to stir himself. The King, it seemed, was furious over the loss of the powder at Portsmouth. He now sharply ordered the General, under pain of his Royal displeasure, to seize every vestige of military supplies which the Colonists had stored up. Also he was to capture the leaders of this rebellion immediately, and he was to ship them to London without fail, to be hanged there as traitors.

It amused me to think of the far-reaching effects of our little ride to Portsmouth that cold winter night: the very King in London driven into a passion, General Gage in disfavor, his troops a laughingstock.

Now the General, smarting under the Royal rebukes, decided to do something big, something really big. He would show them, by Jupiter! In the miserable little village of Concord these stupid rebels were known to have collected a large supply of stores. Very well, he would take them. And right on the way, at Lexington, were reposing two of their most troublesome leaders, John Hancock and that braggart Sam Adams. He would snatch them up as well, by George. Two birds with one stone as 'twere.

A real force this time, at least a thousand men, in charge of Colonel Smith. Good man, Smith; knew his business; second cousin to the Earl of Sleeve, played an excellent hand of whist too. The expedition would go at night, while the clodhoppers slept. The date? Well, April eighteenth seemed as good as any; that would be a Tuesday and Tuesday had always been his lucky day.

But Secrecy! Secrecy was the watchword! This time not a word, not a whisper of his plans should leak out to spoil everything. Like that miserable Portsmouth affair . . .

Poor General Gage! By Saturday the fifteenth Mr. Revere had been fully informed of all these plans. He was talking them over with Colonel Conant while he swept out the stable and fed me.

"The only two points that I am not sure of," Mr. Revere said, "are the exact hour of departure, and whether they will cross by the Neck, or may possibly ferry over to here or to Cambridge."

"Cambridge, I am sure," the Colonel said. "There lies the *Somerset*, newly anchored in midstream. Do you see all the longboats from the rest of the Fleet, freshly calked and strung out behind her? Are those for a picnic or a fishing expedition?" He chuckled. "General Gage does advertise his secrets wonderfully well."

"He does indeed," Mr. Revere agreed, laughing. "The only person in all Boston who doesn't know of his present venture is old Abijah Upshaw, and he has been deaf since birth. I think I shall ride out to Lexington tomorrow, though, and warn Sam Adams and John Hancock, just in case they haven't been told."

"Might as well," the Colonel yawned. "It ought to be a pleasant day. Wouldn't mind going along myself, if I had as fine a horse as yours." He slapped me on the neck. "Give my regards to Sam and John."

Sunday *was* a pleasant day. It was a beautiful day, one of those sudden unseasonably warm days which come so unexpectedly in the New England spring. The grass was now quite green, in sheltered spots early flowers were peeping forth, buds on the trees were beginning to burst.

All the young Reveres were dressed in their Sunday best, ready for church. Little Mary had found a few primroses and braided them into my forelock. Mr. Revere appeared carrying a small package of lunch which he put in his saddlebag. He mounted, took Elizabeth on the saddle before him, and we gave her a ride as far as the corner.

110

It was delightful to be setting out for such a pleasant ride, so different from some of our other trips; no icy gales or frozen ruts to contend with, no need for haste. The little streams were full, on their sunny banks the new grass was deep and lush, water cress was beginning to wave in the clear water. As we jogged along Mr. Revere whistled a few bars from the popular new tune "Yankee Doodle." He was a rather poor whistler, but he was drowned out by the chorus of birds who were now out in full force.

We met many people on the roads — in carriages, carts; on horseback or afoot — all going to services at their meetinghouses. On some of the village greens groups of young men were gathered, laughing or jostling as they waited for the church hour to be over before beginning their drill. We were known to everyone, by sight or reputation, and were greeted cheerily everywhere. Frequently Mr. Revere stopped to gossip with the Militia and the Minute Men, to gather and pass out information.

The whole countryside seemed to know of General Gage's impending raid, but no one was sure of the exact day.

"It is Tuesday night, positively," Mr. Revere assured them.

"Unless it rains," someone guffawed. "They ain't a-goin' to get them pretty uniforms wet. Just you let us know when they start, Mr. Revere, an' we'll be ready for 'em."

We also passed several small parties of British Officers, more than usual, and I wondered whether they were spying out the roads or merely the taverns. They all passed us in stony silence, although many cast curious glances at me, for I did not resemble the usual farm horse. I almost hoped that we might encounter Leftenant Barnstable and Ajax, for it would have given me the greatest pleasure to show that overfed slug how easily I could leave him behind on the open road.

So we pursued our easy way to Lexington, where we found Sam Adams and Mr. Hancock staying at the pleasant home of the Reverend Jonas Clark. It was a delightful scene that we came upon, a far cry from War's threats and alarms. The Clark family and guests had just finished Sunday dinner, evidently a large one. Sam Adams dozed in a hammock, while a very beautiful young lady read aloud to John Hancock. The Reverend Jonas and his wife wandered about the rose garden looking over last winter's damage.

Mr. Revere, I am sure, hated to disrupt this tranquil gathering, but never one to shirk his duty he at once dismounted and attempted to wake Sam Adams. It was quite a task, but once accomplished he poured out his news of the impending raid.

"Yes, yes, Paul my boy," Adams yawned. "We have heard it

112

rumored that the British Lion intends emerging from his foul lair. But are we such cravens as to ignominiously flee at the first whisper of a threat?"

"It is more than a whisper," Mr. Revere answered, "I know it for an absolute fact. The British march Tuesday night. You and Mr. Hancock should not be here. Your lives are far too important to the Cause to be risked in this fashion."

"Thank you for the compliment," Sam Adams said, and yawned again. "But Tuesday is some time off and I find it very pleasant here. We shall depend on you for warning, my fleet-footed courier of the night. Moreover, we are well guarded. All during the dark hours a Corporal and seven valiant Militiamen pace their posts around our peaceful domicile." He sank back in the hammock and resumed his nap.

"But Mr. Hancock . . ." Mr. Revere appealed to Sam's companion. "What are eight men against a thousand British regulars? Besides, I may not be able to get through. What will you do if the British arrive, and you unwarned?"

"Do?" shouted John Hancock. "I shall snatch up the nearest musket and take my place in the ranks beside my fellow Patriots. Who am *I* to shrink from the common danger?"

He looked very noble and the young lady seemed sufficiently impressed. "Do not fear, Mr. Revere," she said soulfully. "The Almighty will watch over them." Then she resumed her reading.

Mr. Revere shrugged helplessly and we started off up the road. It was the closest I have ever seen him to being really angry. "*Snatch up a musket* . . ." he snorted. "And he can't even load one, let alone fire it. *The Almighty will watch over them!* The Almighty and eight Militia boys! Oh well, Sherry, we've done our duty. Now for Concord."

I started up the Concord road on a brisk trot, but halfway there he remembered his lunch. We stopped at a quiet little bridge where he ate his sandwiches while I cropped the fresh spring grass and drank deeply from the clear brook.

Our reception at Concord was vastly different from Lexington's. Here the Committee of Safety were all alert and eager for news. Perhaps they had dined less heartily than Messrs. Adams and Hancock. When Mr. Revere revealed the British plans, they sprang into action at once. Messengers were sent galloping to

114

all the surrounding villages. The Concord Minute Men and Militia set to work breaking out the stores. Sacks of bullets were buried in a nearby orchard. The pitifully few cannon were loaded on farm wagons and started for Groton, Acton and Sudbury. Carts loaded with rations, muskets, powder, cannon balls and medical supplies were sent off in various directions.

Trotting leisurely homeward, we continually met carts escorted by armed Militia all making for Concord to assist in the removal. As we learned later, so well was the work done that by Tuesday evening not so much as a musket ball remained in Concord.

So much for General Gage and his great secret!

After supper Colonel Conant dropped around to hear of our trip. He was delighted with the prompt action of the Concord authorities and amused by the lethargy of Sam Adams and John Hancock.

"Small wonder they're not eager to leave the Reverend Clark's home," he chuckled, "Sam is doubtless eating better than he has in years and it is well known that John is paying court to the handsome young lady you saw. I do hope, though, that he is not so bemused that he'll forget that trunk."

"Trunk?" asked Mr. Revere.

115

"Yes. At the tavern next door he has a small leather trunk that old Gage would give his eyeteeth to lay hands on. It holds the rosters of all the Militia companies and their Officers, lists of all the Patriot leaders — everything. If it ever fell into British hands none of our necks would be worth an old shoe. When you go to warn them Tuesday night make sure that trunk's safe. If those two want to be stubborn — all right, let them be. *But get that trunk!*"

"Indeed I will," Mr. Revere agreed. "I have a certain fondness for my neck in its present shape; I do not care to have it stretched."

"Now as to my plans. I shall stay in Boston tomorrow and Tuesday, getting all possible information. When the British start to move Dr. Warren will send out Will Dawes by way of the Neck. Perhaps he can get by the sentries, perhaps not. The moment we are sure of their route I have arranged with Rob Newman to signal you from Old North. If they are going by the Neck he will hang one lantern in that window there, just below the belfry. If they are ferrying over to Cambridge he will hang two. As soon as you see the signal you'd better get Sherry saddled and ready. Tom Richardson and Josh Bentley will row me over.

"If you hear firing from the *Somerset* or if I'm not here within a half hour, you or Devens will have to ride — I won't be coming."

The two men stood there awhile gazing out at the river, their pipes glowing in the darkness. On the Boston shore the tall spire of Old North could just be seen, the window below the belfry

116

a small dark blob. In midstream lay the dark, threatening bulk of the *Somerset*.

Colonel Conant finally spoke. "You going over tonight?"

"Right away," Mr. Revere answered.

"This is a pretty risky business, Paul," the other said. "Good luck to you." Without more words they shook hands and the Colonel stumped off up the lane.

Mr. Revere bid his family good-by hastily, for he was anxious to get across before the rising of the moon. Just as he started down the path to the shore his mother called, "Oh, Paul dear, this time please remember to bring my small round sewing basket when you come. It is the gray wicker one in the upper left-hand drawer of my lowboy. Now don't forget, the way you usually do."

The strain of the next two days told heavily on everyone. The children got quite out of hand, little Joshua caught a bad cold and Mrs. Revere grieved that she couldn't call in Dr. Warren. Colonel Conant dropped around two or three times a day to see if there was any news from Mr. Revere, although he knew perfectly well there would be none until Tuesday night. Old Mrs. Revere worried about her sewing basket.

Miss Deborah was the calmest of the lot; she fed and watered me and brushed me a dozen times a day. But her troubled eyes often rested on the spire of Old North and on the *Somerset*. In the bright sunlight the church looked very close, the signal window very sharp and clear — and the shining guns of the *Somerset* looked wickedly efficient.

117

Tuesday evening finally came. And before it was scarcely dark there also came Colonel Conant, Richard Devens and several other members of the Committee. The general nervousness had begun to affect even me. I was restless and rather unpleasant when Colonel Conant insisted on saddling and bridling me hours before it was necessary.

"Father said they wouldn't move before the moon rose," Miss Deborah said, somewhat impatiently, "and Father always knows." She loosened my girth and stroked me quietly.

"It's surely Cambridge," someone said. "Ed Whipple was over there this afternoon and there was a scad of Officers, down around the landing place mostly."

Now in the deepening dusk we could see all the longboats being cast off and slowly rowed in to the Boston shore, along where the Common ran down to the water. Mrs. Revere, having put the children to bed, came out and joined the group.

After what seemed hours, the sky in the east began to glow, the buildings of Boston became silhouettes. Slowly the moon

rose, fat and orange; the spire of Old North was a sharp paper cutout.

"There they go," someone cried. Beyond the *Somerset* we could now see the lines of barges and longboats crawling across the river like a procession of huge black beetles. Now and then the moonlight winked on a bayonet or a buckle. The procession seemed endless.

Old North boomed out eleven, and still no signal. Colonel Conant and Richard Devens began to argue as to which should ride — in case —

Their voices stopped abruptly. High up in the dark spire a light flickered a moment, then settled down to a steady clear pinpoint. Seconds later another appeared, far enough separated from the first to show clearly two distinct dots of light.

"By Cambridge," everyone breathed.

If the strain of the last two days had been hard, the next half hour was well-nigh unbearable. Now every eye was fastened on the *Somerset*, black and menacing. The procession of barges still continued. The men paced back and forth, cleared their throats, lit their pipes and let them go out. Miss Deborah braided and unbraided my forelock twenty times.

Still there came no sign of life from the warship; no shouted challenge, no flash or roar of guns.

So intent were we that everyone gave a great start when the bell of Old North clanged out one stroke. Eleven-thirty!

Colonel Conant sighed, settled his hat, and started toward me. "The half hour is up," he said. "I will ride, Devens."

But before he had reached my side there came a bumping and scraping on the shore, a splash and the scramble of footsteps. Miss Deborah yanked my girth tight as Mr. Revere came hurrying up the slope from the water.

With scarcely a word — with only a hurried embrace for his wife and a pat on the cheek for Deborah — he grasped the reins, leaped into the saddle; and we were off.

As we swirled out of the gate in a shower of flying gravel I heard old Mrs. Revere cry, "Oh Paul, Paul. You've been and forgotten my sewing basket *again!*"

## 12.  The Last Ride

Aᴀꜰᴛᴇʀ ᴛʜᴇ sᴛʀᴀɪɴ of the last two
days it was a glorious relief to be in action again. For the first
few miles the road to Lexington led over open moorlands. The
moon was bright, the footing good, and I fairly flew. Later,
when we came to shadowy woodlands, we would have to proceed with more care for fear of ambush. Now was our chance to
make real speed.

Mr. Revere suddenly slapped the pommel, looking for his pistols. "Confound old Conant," he laughed. "No doubt fussing around all evening, being a pest to everyone, and then forgets my pistols. Oh well, never mind, I couldn't hit a barn with them anyway." He too seemed in a high good humor, now that the strain of waiting was past.

As we galloped I was haunted by the recollection of all the British Officers we had seen on the road last Sunday. Surely such an important expedition as this one would have many scouts out watching the roads. I must be unusually wary.

Now we were in more wooded country almost halfway to Lexington and had met no one. As we passed patch after patch of ominous black shadow without a challenge I must have become overconfident or careless. For what happened next I consider myself wholly to blame.

We were approaching a great spreading oak tree that bathed the road in deep shadow when the first thing we knew there was a shout, a rush — and two British Officers burst out of the blackness, blocking our way. I slid to a stop before Mr. Revere had even realized our danger. One Officer wheeled and galloped up the road a space, lest we should escape the first, who was now charging down on us with drawn pistol.

In a split second I recognized him as Leftenant Barnstable, mounted on Ajax!

Ajax, I am sure, meant to run me down, but at the last instant I skipped aside just enough to escape his heavy charge and the Leftenant's snatch at my bridle. We were now fairly trapped, one Officer ahead of us, one behind.

Furious at my carelessness, I whirled, sprang and cleared the
stone wall beside the road. It was only a low wall and I made my
landing as gentle as possible, but was terrified lest Mr. Revere

be unseated. He was — almost. He fell forward heavily on my neck, lost one stirrup, scrambled frantically for a moment and then, praise be, somehow managed to right himself.

We were in a huge open field, dotted here and there with boulders and clumps of bayberry, but excellent footing. Now I could show this pompous, overstuffed barracks brute what running really was! I let myself out and skimmed the ground like a racing cloud shadow. Far behind I could hear Ajax crashing through the brush, thundering over the wall, pounding across the rolling field. I could easily have outdistanced him, dived into the woods and lost him completely, but that would have wasted time and I had a better plan.

Now I was duly thankful for my thorough knowledge of the countryside. For I remembered that that dark mass of trees and brush near the far side of the field overhung a deep stagnant pond. I also remembered that on this side the ground dropped in a steep gravelly bank to the water. I made for it, slowing my pace to allow Ajax to catch up. Mr. Revere knew of the pond also, but wisely he left everything in my hands, making no attempt to hasten my now slow pace or to guide me in any way.

Ajax was almost on my heels; I could hear his laboring breath, could smell the stale stable odor of his saddle blanket. With a roar the Leftenant's pistol went off. The bullet whined harmlessly past my left ear.

Not until we reached the very brink did I wheel in a sharp right-angled turn. Mr. Revere must have sensed it coming, for to my great relief he managed somehow to cling on.

As we sped off across the field there came to our ears a most gratifying sound: a heavy crashing of bushes, the ring of iron-shod shoes on sliding cobbles, a screamed volley of oaths, then a tremendous splash.

There flashed through my mind those bitter words: *I never speak to civilians. . . . Deserter! Traitor! Spy!* I burst out in a long derisive whinny. Slapping me on the shoulder, Mr. Revere shouted: "Good girl, Sherry. Well done. One down and Concord to go."

We found an open barway and were out on a small back-country road. I recognized it at once as being close to Medford. In a few moments we rattled across the wooden bridge spanning the Mystic River and bore down on the sleeping town.

We paused only a moment at the door of Mr. Doolittle the sheep raiser. Mr. Revere set up a great pounding, shouting, "The Redcoats are out! Turn out Minute Men!" Before the echoes of his first knock had died away Enoch Sawtell, the shepherd, came briskly forth, fully dressed and carrying his musket. He fired it once in the air and with only a wave to us ran for the meeting-house.

As we galloped down the short village street lights were springing up in all the houses, the steady thudding of an alarm drum began and the meetinghouse bell burst into a wild clangor. Medford was well awake.

The encounter with the British Officers had forced us considerably out of our way, losing much precious time. However, the road from Medford to Lexington was so small and little used that we doubted it was being watched. Watched or not, ambush or no ambush, we must now press on with all possible speed,

125

regardless of danger. I settled down to a steady ground-consuming gallop and ran as though I were competing for the King's Cup.

Farmhouses were few; when we passed one Mr. Revere would shout at the top of his lungs, "Turn out Minute Men! The British are out!" This and my pounding hoofs were usually enough to set all the dogs to barking and rouse the household.

Only once did we pause. At the top of a high open rise Mr. Revere drew rein and for a brief moment we looked and listened. Behind us we could see almost every hilltop crowned with a blazing beacon fire. Far and near the meetinghouse bells kept up an unceasing clamor that spread ever westward. Here and there could be heard the rattle of a drum, occasionally a musket shot.

I found my heart beating harder than the exercise warranted. All our other trips, while necessary and important to the cause, had really been mere messenger service, political junkets; no ambushes, no blazing pistols. But this was War, bloody War, or perilously close to it.

I remembered the never-ending procession of boats filled with well-trained British troops. Even now the close-ranked columns

were on the march. I thought of Enoch Sawtell — his grim hatred of the scarlet uniform, the speed with which the whole village of Medford had flown to arms. I remembered how promptly and efficiently the men of Concord had plunged into the work of removing their stores last Sunday. Perhaps these Minute Men and Militia were not so comic as they had seemed. I could still see those white corncobs flipping into the air — *These men can shoot.*

Mr. Revere slapped my neck and I resumed my gallop. The soft dirt road was delightful underfoot, the moon was bright, great trees here and there cast black shadows any of which might conceal a lurking scout. But I had now cast aside all thought of scouts or ambushes. My one thought was speed — and Lexington.

Then all unexpectedly we were there, racing across the village green. Evidently we had outdistanced the alarm bells; the

127

town was wrapped in deepest slumber. The Militia Corporal on guard at the Jonas Clark home smoked his pipe, the sentries sleepily walked their posts.

"Turn out, turn out!" Mr. Revere roared at the top of his voice. "The Regulars are on the march!" His voice echoed down the street. The Corporal knocked out his pipe and advanced angrily.

"Stop that hullabaloo," he shouted. "I got strict orders the gentlemen's not to be disturbed."

"They'll be disturbed enough shortly," Mr. Revere exploded, "when the British get here." The sentries all left their posts and gathered around.

"I got strict orders — " the Corporal began again, but Mr. Revere impatiently rode past him up to the front door and beat a thunderous tattoo on the knocker. All around the green candles were beginning to show in the houses. Finally lights began to stir in the parsonage, a window was raised and John Hancock stuck his head out. "Is that you, Revere?" he called. "Step right in."

Mr. Revere dismounted and went in. Lights were showing now all over the house, there were running footsteps and much confusion. I could hear Mr. Revere's voice giving out his news, loud yawns from Sam Adams, John Hancock calling for his sword and uniform, arguments and some weeping.

Suddenly Mr. Hancock burst forth from the front door, a uniform coat half-buttoned over his nightshirt, an old sword strapped on all awry, his feet encased in carpet slippers and a cotton nightcap still perched on his head. The beautiful young lady and Mrs. Clark were weeping and pleading with him.

128

"To arms!" he declaimed. "Where is my musket? Where is the enemy? Where are my papers? Where is my secretary?"

Sam Adams and the Reverend Mr. Clark now joined the ladies in persuading Mr. Hancock to moderate his military ardor. He gave in rather promptly. "Oh well," he said resignedly. "If you *all* insist" — and unstrapped his sword. "At least we have time for breakfast." Sam Adams enthusiastically seconded that idea and Mr. Revere reluctantly agreed.

The whole village was now astir. Captain Parker of the Minute Men lined up his little troop on the green, messengers were sent hither and yon, the beacon on a nearby hill was set blazing, the meetinghouse bell clanged steadily. Mr. Clark's light chaise was driven around to the front door.

In the midst of the confusion a rider galloped up, his poor lathered mount in the last stages of exhaustion. It was Mr. William Dawes, whom Dr. Warren had sent out before us by way of the Neck. Mr. Revere rushed out, greeted him and dragged him into the house for a bite of breakfast.

The horse, a pleasant but rather homely country nag, stumbled over to where I was munching a basket of oats. "Do you mind?" she asked, eying my water bucket wistfully.

"Not at all," I replied. "Help yourself, my dear — but not too much, I would advise. After the run you have had it would be quite unwise." I pushed my pannier of oats over to her. "A little food would no doubt be welcome too." She ate and drank sparingly, but most gratefully. Gradually her heaving sides quieted down, the trembling of her legs grew less.

"Whew," she finally sighed. "That *were* a gallop for fair. I surely am dead-beat. And after all that pother you beat us here anyway. Reck'n I wasn't ever built for speed. Haulin' a plow and helpin' with the hay gives you strength all right, but not the runnin' kind. Well, I done my best and that's all any horse kin do."

"Don't give it a thought," I said consolingly. "You two had a

130

much greater distance to travel and you arrived here almost as soon as we did. It was a splendid performance. Just suppose we hadn't gotten through, as we almost didn't — you would have saved the day." She was much pleased by my words and perked up considerably.

There now ensued a period of great confusion while Messrs. Adams and Hancock prepared to depart. They, the Clark family and servants, rushed in and out of the house bringing out various items of luggage and storing them in the chaise. Young Lowell, Mr. Hancock's secretary, arrived and tried to take down numerous letters and notes which Mr. Hancock shouted at him above the din of the meetinghouse bell. Then it was discovered that Mr. Hancock was still wearing his nightshirt under his uniform coat, so his bag had to be extracted and returned to the house, where he changed into more conventional attire.

All this time Mr. Revere kept reminding Mr. Hancock and Sam Adams of the invaluable trunk of papers, but was always brushed aside with, "Yes, yes, young Lowell will attend to that." The distracted Lowell, for his part, always answered, "Yes, yes, that will be attended to."

Suddenly Mr. Dawes asked if Concord had been warned, but in the general confusion no one seemed to know. Captain Parker *thought* someone had been sent. The Corporal of the Guard was sure no one had left; Sam Adams didn't know anything about it and Mr. Hancock was still changing his clothes.

Rather irritably Mr. Revere threw himself into the saddle, Mr. Dawes followed suit, and we started off for Concord at the best pace we could manage. Very shortly we overtook a young man

131

mounted on a rather good-looking, fresh horse. He introduced himself as Dr. Samuel Prescott of Concord, a High Son of Liberty. It seemed that he had been spending the night with friends in Lexington. Wakened by the alarm, he was now hurrying home and would be glad to join forces with us. As he knew all the roads and byways, he was a welcome addition to our company.

Mr. Dawes's poor horse was now so exhausted that we had to moderate our pace somewhat, but it was only six miles to Concord and we were now about halfway there. So busy were the three men rousing the farmhouses that we passed and so concerned about Mr. Dawes's horse that they completely forgot the possibility of an ambush. It was an unfortunate moment to be forgetful.

Suddenly from the shadow of the trees there came another rush, a volley of oaths — and this time we found ourselves confronted by four King's Officers, all with pistols drawn. None of our party was armed; the road was too narrow to wheel and attempt flight. We were fairly caught, and Concord but three miles away!

The Officers herded us through an open barway into a large pasture where we were met by two more. They were now six to our three. Our plight seemed hopeless, but I heard young Dr. Prescott whisper to Mr. Revere, "When we pass that bayberry bush, bolt. I will go right, you left." As we approached the dark clump my heart quickened. I summoned my last remaining energy for one crucial effort.

"*Now!*" roared the Doctor and plunged his spurs into his

mount's flanks. The spirited young horse whirled as though stung, cleared a high stone wall with a magnificent leap and was tearing up the road to Concord before the sluggish Britons had gathered their wits.

The moment I heard the Doctor's *now* I wheeled to the left and set off across the pasture at top speed. In the open we offered a fair mark; there were several pistol shots but no ball came near us. My weariness had left me, I galloped like mad; the thundering British chargers fell farther and farther behind.

I was making for a dark patch of woodland. Once we had gained that, I knew we could easily lose our pursuers. We were almost there, I was beginning to breathe easier. Mr. Revere slapped my shoulder in relief — when out of the woodland trotted six more armed Officers.

Now we *were* caught, hopelessly caught. Our pursuers came galloping up and we were surrounded by ten Britishers, each with a pistol pointed at Mr. Revere's breast. I was utterly exhausted and disheartened; my flanks heaved, my head drooped. I could feel Mr. Revere slump dispiritedly in the saddle.

Someone thought to inquire about the third prisoner, but no one seemed to know anything about him. In their excited pursuit of me he had been completely forgotten. Left alone and unguarded in the middle of the pasture, Mr. Dawes apparently had just walked his tired mount away.

I now recognized the Officer in charge as my old commander, Colonel Dalrymple. His face purple with rage at the escape of the two prisoners, he began to question Mr. Revere roughly.

"What is your name, yokel?" he demanded.

Mr. Revere straightened in the saddle. "Paul Revere," he answered proudly.

"Revere? Revere?" Sir Dagmore choked. "Revere the courier, Revere the spy!" Then he broke into a loud roar of laughter.

"Egad, men, we *have* snared a prize! Won't the General be pleased when we bring *him* into Boston! Revere the spy! Promotions all round, no doubt. Commendations no end!"

"You will never see Boston," Mr. Revere said calmly.

"What's that, what's that?" the Colonel sputtered. "Never see Boston?"

"Your troops were stranded by the tide crossing the river,"

134

Mr. Revere continued. "They never reached Cambridge. And I have roused all the countryside between here and Boston. There are five hundred Minute Men at Lexington now and more coming every moment. Every road is filled with them — you are cut off, surrounded. Just listen."

In the momentary silence that followed there could be heard the clanging of innumerable meetinghouse bells. The sky glowed with the glare of signal beacons ever growing nearer. Now and then came the sound of a musket shot or the far-off tattoo of a drum.

"Damme," Sir Dagmore growled, "the rascally clodhopper may be telling the truth for once. Sergeant Dobbins, take his horse; yours is done in. The prisoner will walk, and see that you keep a good watch on him. If *he* escapes someone will be cashiered for this stupid night's work."

The heavy Sergeant heaved himself into the saddle and we proceeded rather aimlessly southward. But as we approached the first road there could be heard the noisy approach of a band of Militia. We waited in the shadows until they had passed and then started northward. We had proceeded almost to Lexington when there crashed out a loud volley of musketry directly ahead.

The startled mounts began milling around, the Officers lost their heads; and soon our party was in complete confusion. Although I knew it was only a signal volley, I misbehaved worse than the rest. I reared and plunged, charging among the others. I doubled the confusion, although the Sergeant yanked my bit and spurred me cruelly. Suddenly Sir Dagmore's voice bellowed above the uproar: "*The prisoner,* where is the prisoner?"

The prisoner was gone. At the height of the confusion I had seen Mr. Revere step quietly into the bushes bordering the field. By now he must be well on his way to Lexington.

"A fine night's work!" the Colonel raged. "We start with three prisoners and their mounts; now what have we? One scurvy, ill-begotten country nag. A splendid present for the General, that. He will appreciate it, I am sure."

Once more we started our fruitless wandering, now south, now west, now east. Each time we approached a road or village something occurred to alarm our now panicky Officers and we started off in a different direction. This continued for a half hour or more.

The smell of army stables and barracks clung to everything: the horses, their saddles and blankets, even the men's uniforms. It fairly sickened me. The heavy-handed Sergeant, his callous use of bit and spur, the pompous stupidity of the Officers, all served to sink me into utmost gloom. I was back in the Army again, my new-found freedom was a lost dream, never to be regained.

I was frantic to escape, but what chance had I? I was thoroughly exhausted, the Sergeant was a good rider; even should I manage to rid myself of him and attempt to run for it, any of the Officers would shoot me without a thought.

All unexpectedly my salvation arrived in the form of three white blurs slowly moving in single file along the edge of a brush-bordered lane. Of course these city- and barracks-bred Britons did not realize their significance, but in my many travels with Mr. Revere I had often encountered these North American

136

skunks and had acquired the greatest respect for their prowess. Day or night, I knew a skunk when I saw one. Now I was delighted to see that Colonel Dalrymple's heavy-footed horse was about to step on the leading one. He never did.

I saw the three white blurs suddenly rise erect and quiver slightly. Then with a squeal of pain the half-blinded, maddened mount reared and whirled, throwing the Colonel heavily. Several of the other horses and their riders were well sprayed. The Officers choked, wept and shouted, their mounts plunged, reared and kicked. A nauseating stench rose to the heavens. The volley of musketry had thrown the party into confusion, but the skunk's volleys were even more devastating.

With the Colonel's fall my Sergeant started to dismount to go to his aid. I helped him off with a stiff-legged buck. As he fell to the ground he still clung to the reins, but I lashed out viciously; he dropped the reins, rolled over and covered his head with his arms.

I was a free horse again!

I made for the lane, but just as I reached the edge of the thicket there came the roar and flash of a pistol, and this time the ball did not miss. I felt a paralyzing blow on my left shoulder, as though I had been kicked by Ajax. For a moment

137

I thought I was going down, but somehow managed to scramble through the bushes and stumble out into the lane. Luckily the Officers were too occupied to give chase.

At first my shoulder and foreleg seemed merely numb, but as I hobbled along the numbed feeling gradually changed to one of intense pain. I was sure that no bone was broken, but I was bleeding profusely. I could feel the hot blood running down my foreleg.

I knew that the lane led to Lexington, so I made the best progress I could in that direction. Surely Mr. Revere would have gone there. As I stumbled along, the sky in the east grew steadily lighter; by the time I saw the first houses the sun was about to rise. A before-dawn mist shrouded everything.

The village seemed still and deserted — doubtless the men were all out with the Militia, the women and children hidden indoors. Through the low-hanging mist I could make out a dark mass of Minute Men gathered on the green.

I was in an orchard at the rear of the inn. As I approached the building, Mr. Revere and young Lowell staggered through the back door, lugging between them a leather trunk.

I whinnied weakly.

At the sound Mr. Revere looked up, dropped the trunk and with a glad shout ran toward me.

## 13. Warrior's Return

**M**R. REVERE was aghast when he
saw my injury. He dropped to his knees in the wet grass, probed
and examined my wound. When he rose his face was white and
drawn, his hands covered with my blood. Without a word he
rushed into the inn to return in a moment with a clean sheet.

"Mr. Revere," young Lowell called, "what about the trunk?"

"Blast the trunk," shouted Mr. Revere. "I warned you and I

warned Sam Adams and I warned Hancock. If you're all three stupid enough to forget it, that's your misfortune. I'm a courier, not a porter."

He ran to the well and returned with a bucket of icy cold water. He washed my wound carefully, tore the sheet into strips and bandaged it as tightly as possible. The bleeding lessened considerably, the cold water was most soothing. He gave me a small drink, then threw my reins over an apple branch.

"There now, Sherry," he said, stroking my neck, "just wait here quietly until I help hide this idiotic trunk." He angrily snatched up one end of the trunk and started off at a pace so furious that it had young Lowell stumbling and half running to keep up. They disappeared around the back of the meeting-house and I was left alone in the quiet orchard. Slowly the mist was burned away by the newly risen sun.

Then my heart stopped a second as far down the road I heard the old familiar thudding of drums, the squealing of fifes. The drums grew louder and closer. All at once, the van of the British force burst into view, marching as though on parade; red coats brilliant in the sunlight, buckles and bayonets twinkling, legs rising and falling in a thunderous rhythm that seemed to shake the very ground and sent a great cloud of dust billowing skyward. At the head rode handsome young Major Pitcairn, mounted on a spirited charger that danced and caracoled in time with the music.

The meetinghouse shut off my view of what happened on the green, for which I was deeply thankful. I could see the column halt and two platoons deploy across the green. In the sudden silence I could clearly hear Major Pitcairn's arrogant voice, as he commanded the little band of Minute Men to disperse. Two or three random shots rang out and then were drowned in the great roar of a volley. The King's troops gave a loud huzzah and a thick cloud of black smoke rolled across the road, blotting out everything. When the smoke had cleared the column was again on the move up the Concord road.

After that first volley women and old people rushed forth from the houses to aid the wounded and carry away the dead. Regardless of the stolidly tramping troops or the possibility of more fighting, they went calmly on with their work. I could see many limp forms being borne on shutters into the various houses.

Still the red-clad column continued to pass steadily, seemingly endless, drums thudding, boots thumping, the dust rising ever thicker. The ceaseless passing made me dizzy; the huge numbers of this force made me heartsick when I thought of our small, half-trained Militia bands daring to oppose them.

Then Mr. Revere arrived, gathered up my reins and started to lead me away. He never even looked at the passing troops, his entire interest was concentrated on me. "Well, Sherry," he said, slapping my neck gently. "Our work is done. Now for home. Take it easy, girl, it's a long walk."

The wait had stiffened my leg; and for a while I limped frightfully. I realized, and Mr. Revere did too, that I must keep moving. If we stopped for too long I might never get started again. We kept to the fields and woods, well away from the British-infested road. The hot sun and the exercise limbered me up somewhat and I was able to walk a little better, although

the pain was as bad as ever. Mr. Revere was touchingly kind and thoughtful, pausing occasionally when I grew too tired, picking the easiest paths, encouraging and cheering me on. Whenever we came to a clear fresh stream he changed my bandages, let me drink a bit and cool my hoofs in the water. We would rest only a few moments and then limp on.

We usually kept the road in sight. The British column had long since passed. The rear of the column had consisted of a large number of baggage wagons, evidently intended to carry away the loot from Concord. The dust clouds had drifted away and the road was now empty, save for an occasional galloping courier.

It must have been early afternoon when we became aware of heavy firing back in the direction of Lexington. The firing grew rapidly louder, then we were astonished to see a mounted British Officer come galloping down the road at top speed. His hat was lost, his hair flying loose, both he and his mount were caked from head to heel with black mud. Despite the mud I recognized him as Leftenant Sir Cedric Barnstable. Ajax was limping and thor-

oughly blown, but the Leftenant used whip and spur unmerci-
fully. A moment later several supply wagons raced by, swaying
and clattering.

Then came the British troops — *running!* Running frantically
back toward Boston. Many had lost their shakos, most had
thrown away their muskets, haversacks and everything else that
might impede their progress. *King's troops running!* The shock
and surprise almost prostrated me.

Mr. Revere could not take it in for a moment; his mouth hung
open, he stared unbelievingly at the road. Then suddenly he
clapped me on the back, leaped in the air and emitted a wild
Indian war whoop.

"They run, Sherry! They run!" he howled. "The Regulars are
fleeing! They run like a flock of foolish sheep chased by dogs!"

Farther back the column had a little more semblance of order.
We could see the swords of Officers flashing as they rose and
fell, trying vainly to beat their terrified men into obedience. But
though the close-packed ranks retained their formation the

men would not pause to fight, but continued to tramp as rapidly as possible back toward Cambridge and the protecting guns of their Fleet.

Now we became aware of our Colonials. Racing along through fields and woodlands, ducking and dodging behind trees, boulders, stumps or stone walls, they kept up a deadly accurate fire into the massed scarlet ranks.

They ran singly, in small groups, in larger bands. There were old grandfathers who had fought in the Indian Wars — young lads who had never heard a musket fired in anger. None had uniforms; they were sweat-soaked, dust-caked, powder-blackened

— but they could shoot! Could shoot and take cover. The scattered crackling of their muskets did not sound impressive compared to the roaring British volleys — but red-coated figures kept slumping into the dusty road, Officers dropped from their mounts, wounded horses reared and plunged through the ranks, while our men seldom suffered a scratch.

Only the British rear guard under Colonel Smith still retained some discipline. Now and then they would make a stand, firing futile volleys into the woods and hillsides, while the few remaining baggage wagons hastily gathered up dead and wounded. The tide of battle swirled on down the road, leaving us alone again. Both of us were stunned and shaken. In my weakened state the whole incredible scene seemed like a nightmare. His Royal Majesty's troops routed by a pack of country yokels! Running like rabbits! The pompous warrior Ajax and his precious Leftenant fleeing like panic-stricken cattle!

Mr. Revere came out of his daze, undid my saddle at once and tossed it under a bush. "A lesson I have learned from the British, Sherry," he laughed, "rid yourself of excess weight. Besides we won't need it any more. I shall never ride again."

We resumed our stumbling, limping journey. Being rid of the heavy saddle was some relief, but the sun was now broiling hot, streams were less frequent and there was almost no shade. I grew weaker steadily, the pain was worse, every step was agony. The bed sheet had all been used up. Mr. Revere took off his shirt, tore it into strips and put on one final bandage.

He laughed wryly as we hobbled along. "A fine-looking pair of warriors we are, Sherry," he said. And indeed he looked to be in almost as bad shape as I. He was unshaven, his shirt gone, his hat lost, his hair all awry. His face was scratched, his clothes torn by brush and briers. He was pale from exhaustion, weak and stumbling. He had ridden at breakneck speed all the previous night, twice escaped the British, had carried a heavy trunk a long distance and now had walked all day tending and shepherding me. Except for the hasty breakfast at the Reverend Mr. Clark's, he had not eaten in all that time. Yet he still retained enough

146

spirit to laugh and joke with me and to encourage my faltering footsteps.

Toward sunset we had to cross the dusty road — and a strange sight it was. There were a great many farm wagons; some, their beds cushioned with hay, bore the wounded, both ours and British, others were piled high with muskets, haversacks, canteens and other equipment thrown away by the Regulars in their mad flight.

Among the wounded we saw Enoch Sawtell, the shepherd. He was sitting up and in high good spirits, having only suffered a slight leg wound. He hailed Mr. Revere enthusiastically, holding up his musket and pointing out four notches newly cut in the stock. "Only four," he laughed. "I'm still not the equal of my men when it comes to shooting, but I'm learning. Had a fair shot at that blasted Leftenant Barnstable too, but I only winged him. He were going too fast — back Boston way."

We left the road, which was dusty and depressing, and continued on through the fields. For the remainder of the journey I must have been slightly delirious, for I seemed to be frolicking in the soft green meadows of Sussex, where I spent my earliest days. Strangely enough all the Revere children seemed to be there too, running and playing, gathering armfuls of flowers, stroking my neck affectionately, braiding my forelock.

When I became conscious again all the Revere children *were* there, stroking me gently, speaking endearingly, weeping over my hurts. But I was in my stable in Charlestown. The whole family was gathered there as well as Colonel Conant and, wonder of wonders, Dr. Warren.

147

He, it seemed, by some great good fortune, had managed that evening to get out to Charlestown to treat little Joshua's cold. Now this great and famous Boston physician stripped off his coat, rolled up his sleeves and, kneeling in the stable litter, began to minister to me. All during this long, painful process Miss Deborah held my head, patted me and whispered encouragingly in my ear. Mr. Revere assisted the doctor, Mrs. Revere and the old lady brought linen bandages, lint and steaming bowls of water, while Colonel Conant held the candles.

Skillfully and with as little pain as possible, Dr. Warren opened the wound, cleansed it thoroughly and removed the ugly leaden ball. Then, with the greatest care, he sewed together torn ligaments and muscles and stitched the flaps of skin together as neatly as any housewife.

"There," he finally pronounced as he washed his hands, "I think she will do. She is very weak from loss of blood and will require a great deal of care. Above all, she must not lie down or she may never get up again."

Despite his own exhaustion, and with utter disregard of the frowning guard ships, Mr. Revere strode down to the shore, untied his skiff and rowed off toward Boston. Within an hour he was back, accompanied by the kindly farrier.

The latter at once took charge. He covered my wound with some sweet-smelling, cooling salve; he washed me, rubbed me and brushed me. He kneaded and massaged every muscle, even cleaned and soaked my hoofs, all the while humming softly. The eastern sky was growing gray before he desisted and I at once fell into a sound and refreshing slumber.

148

For ten days he never left the stable, sleeping on the hay and having his meals brought out. Three or four times a day he would lead me slowly around the back yard so as to keep my leg from stiffening.

At the end of his stay he stood out before the stable with Mr. Revere, both of them watching the golden sunset light playing on the buildings of Boston across the river.

"She's still a good horse, Mr. Revere," the farrier said, "but she'll never run again; not the way you had to run her."

Mr. Revere threw his arm over my neck and continued to look out across the river.

"That works out perfectly for both of us," he said with a smile. "She will never run again and I will never ride again. I couldn't bear to ride any other horse; besides, I never liked riding anyway. Sherry has suffered the first wound and shed the first blood in our War of Independence. I think that entitles her to an honorable retirement. From now on she will never again feel the weight of a saddle but will live on the fat of the land. Our despatch-boy days are over and done with."

## Postscript

THE WAR dragged on its long course, but Mr. Revere and I were little involved in it. In June we were warned to leave Charlestown, which we did very promptly, and wisely, for a few days later occurred the bloody battle of Bunker Hill and Charlestown was burned to ashes. In that same battle our beloved Dr. Warren laid down his life. The loss of this dear friend saddened Mr. Revere for many a day. The next little Revere was named Joseph Warren Revere.

One of the happiest days of my life came when the British Forces finally evacuated Boston on March 17, 1776. As the red-clad troops marched down to their ships on the east side of the town, the joyous inhabitants swarmed in from the west side. We stood at the top of a hill looking down the long street to the wharves where the troops were embarking.

Suddenly I saw a horse being hauled up to the yardarm and lowered into the black hold of a transport. It was Ajax. He had proved a false friend, a stupid and bitter enemy, but remembering the horrors of those transports perhaps I should have been moved to feel some pity for him. . . . I was not moved, but whinnied long and gleefully.

It was delightful to be once more in my old stable with its window looking into the kitchen, but we were not destined to be there very long. With Boston free and the War far removed, trade boomed. Mr. Revere's fame as a silversmith spread far and wide, and he soon became highly prosperous. The family moved to a larger home and this farm where I now reside was purchased, chiefly, I suspect, for my benefit.

So here in the lush pastures and the immaculate stable I spend my quiet days. The most joyous time of year comes in early spring, when the family moves out from Boston for the summer. From then until fall I am always surrounded by a half-dozen loving little Reveres. Miss Deborah and the older ones I first knew are quite grown-up now, but there are always new ones arriving.

I have other visitors too. Often, of a Sunday, Hezekiah walks out from the city and spends an afternoon with me. Although he is still fragrant of the glue factory I always enjoy his silent presence. Enoch Sawtell, now a prosperous farmer in his own right, comes now and then, bringing a basket of beautiful apples for me and sometimes too a choice leg of lamb for the family.

Even Sam Adams and Mr. Hancock find time from their important duties with the new Government to visit Mr. Revere now and again. They always insist on coming out to the stable to see me, and Sam Adams has often promised that the Congress, at his demand, will someday award me a medal for my services, but so far nothing has come of it. For my part I much prefer Enoch Sawtell's apples.

Mr. Revere was quite right when he said that his riding days were over. Never since that day has he sat a horse. He did, however, procure a beautiful little light trap in which, on a fine day, he occasionally drives me in to Boston. Despite my slight limp and the two scars which faintly mar my coat I think I can safely say that there are few turnouts in the city equal to ours in dash and elegance.

Sometimes on these occasions I am amused to think of the old hard days when we galloped over those very cobbles at breakneck speed, in rain, snow, sleet, biting cold or blazing heat. They were hard, rough days, and nights, but never, either then or now, have I once regretted that day when I declared my independence and cast in my lot with the champions of Liberty and Freedom.

THE END